Home Again
A Pilgrimage of Father and Son

By

Ron McDonald

© 2002 by Ron McDonald. All rights reserved.

No part of this book may be reproduced, restored in a retrieval system, or transmitted by means, electronic, mechanical, photocopying, recording, or otherwise, without written consent from the author.

ISBN: 0-7596-8432-4 (Ebook)
ISBN: 0-7596-8433-2 (Softcover)

This book is printed on acid free paper.

1stBooks - rev. 04/22/02

Dedicated to my Dad,
who just might be a saint.

Contents

Chapter One – Conflict and Courage in a Southern Town	1
Chapter Two - I'm Not Like my Dad	9
Chapter Three – I Hope This Isn't Just Some Father-Son Bonding Crap	14
Chapter Four - Ozark	32
Chapter Five – Up on the Roof	55
Chapter Six - Illness	61
Chapter Seven – On the Road Again to Pocahontas	70
Chapter Eight - Dewitt	85
Chapter Nine - Rogers	93
About The Author	119

Chapter One

CONFLICT AND COURAGE IN A SOUTHERN TOWN

When I was twelve years old I lived in DeWitt, Arkansas, a small town in the flatlands of the Mississippi River Delta of southeastern Arkansas. Rice was the king crop around DeWitt. Mosquitoes, water moccasins, and rice were everywhere. For a twelve year old boy in DeWitt the world was made up of autumn football, winter basketball, and spring and summer baseball, punctuated by a diversion called school.

My father was the Methodist minister in the town. It was a very friendly town as Southern towns usually are. We developed friends rapidly there. My dad made three best friends who remained so throughout his life: Barnes Hampton, the owner of the local drug store, Jack Essex, the owner of the funeral home, and Pat Patillo, who sold insurance. I made friends from the LaFargue family, who virtually adopted me that first summer we were there. Their father, Quinn LaFargue, II, was an active leader in the church and would take Dad fishing.

I especially remember Johnny and Lucree Schallhorn. He was to take over his dad's hardware store and, together, they were the Methodist Youth Fellowship sponsors. They were the only grown-ups I knew who insisted that we call them by their first names.

DeWitt was a nice place to live. At least it was for white people.

This was during the 1960s, at the height of the civil rights movement. Sometimes waves from the civil rights movement would roll through the small towns in the

South. One of those waves rolled through DeWitt, Arkansas. Two rumors began to make noise through our social network: the "colored folks", it was said, were going to march on the white churches or, God forbid, the swimming pool. Conversation centered around when they might do this, and which they would confront? The church or the swimming pool? White folks were worried.

One Monday evening at the Official Board meeting of our Methodist Church, during those rumor fed days, someone stood up and, after being recognized by the Chair, Mr. Essex, said, "I move that if colored people come to this church, we instruct the ushers to turn them away and tell them where the colored churches are."

The motion was quickly seconded, and discussion followed. It became evident fairly quickly that my father was not in favor of the passage of this motion. In fact, he volunteered that he would stand in the way of it.

In the Methodist Church, the minister of a church has veto power that can only be overridden by the bishop. Members of the Board, therefore knew that should my father veto their decision, any possible override would have to go through channels to the bishop. It would be a major problem. So they decided to table the motion for a month, to be voted on at the next Official Board meeting. In the meantime, everyone knew that the month would be a time to convince the preacher to go along with what the community wanted.

The meeting adjourned and the politicking began.

Up until then baseball, basketball, and football had been all I thought life was about. But we began to feel something new. Something strange was happening. Even in our youth group, Johnny and Lucree were concerned about something as well. We didn't know what it was, though. I was only 12. I didn't understand.

Home Again

One night at supper, all of my family was together: me, my brothers, and Mother and Dad. Dad said to us, "Boys, I want you to know about something that is going on right now."

We all perked up, knowing this would explain something of what we had been feeling.

Dad said, "There are some people in our church who would not like colored people to be able to worship with us should they decide they would like to. They say that if colored people come to our church the ushers should turn them away at the door."

We sat there a bit, waiting, until one of my brothers asked, "Well, Daddy, what do you think?"

He replied, "If Jesus were one of our ushers, what do you think Jesus would do?"

I remember that no one answered that question. We sat there quietly. We knew the answer, and we knew what Dad's answer would be, and his answer was becoming ours at that moment.

Now we knew what was really happening.

On the Sunday before the Monday meeting of the Official Board, the church was packed. Our small sanctuary that usually had 200 people, must have had 300. People love controversy, and this was more than sports and farming. Everyone knew this was important. We wanted to know what would happen, and this was the Sunday to be there!

I remember it well. What Dad said was over my head intellectually, but I remember the unusual quietness of the congregation. Sometimes when people are moved they raise their voices. Sometimes when people are stirred, they lean forward in utter silence. The Spirit was moving the people to silence that day. I could feel that Spirit settling the people down into a reflective mode they hadn't been in before. I didn't understand what Dad was talking about, but I remember seeing him choked up, straining to keep his composure as he spoke. I remember the 12 year old prayer that I prayed as I watched this man, my father. I prayed, "God, please help my daddy not to cry in public and embarrass me."

But I watched him. I watched him like an eagle. He suddenly ended his sermon, and looked at a congregation that was quieter than I'd ever experienced before. It was time for him to say his usual closing prayer, invite people to commit themselves to Christian discipleship or membership in our church, and direct us to turn into our hymnals to a particular numbered hymn. Instead, he stood before that congregation that was quiet and still as could be, surveyed these people we knew so well, and announced firmly, "You are dismissed!"

Then, instead of walking to the rear of the church where we would all file out, he turned towards his study next to the choir loft behind him, and walked out of the sanctuary, leaving the congregation in stunned silence.

We could have heard a pin drop on the rug. We hardly breathed.

Then someone stood up, others did, and without the usual raised voices, we filed quietly out of church.

I wanted to see more of what was going on, so I got up and walked up to my daddy's study. There he was, standing behind his desk. He must have been talking with Mr. Essex who sang in the choir. He stood with his hands holding onto both sides of that desk, gripping it as if he was having trouble standing up.

I backed out of there, knowing it wasn't a place for a 12 year old. Years later I asked my dad what he was feeling at that moment. This man whom I had idealized as a person of great courage said, "I was scared to death."

Home Again

The Official Board met the next night. It also was a full house. No one who could come would miss this meeting. Mr. Essex, Mr. Hampton, Mr. Patillo, Johnny Schallhorn, Mr. LaFargue—they were all there. Dad was there, too, and he had let it be known that he would stick with his decision to veto any action to close our church to any person, regardless of race. He also had garnered the support of the bishop, who would not override his veto. The confrontation was set. With a vote in favor of the motion, and the subsequent veto, the church might be split wide apart.

Mr. Essex, the Chair, called the meeting to order. Immediately two men stood up—one was Mr. Hampton—and shouted, "Mr. Chairman!"

Mr. Essex recognized "Mr. Hampton."

Mr. Hampton said, "I move the meeting be adjourned."

Mr. Patillo stood and shouted, "Second!"

Parlimentary procedures require that a motion and second to adjourn be voted on immediately. It passed. The split was avoided.

Mr. LaFargue stormed out of the church and did not come back to church as long as my dad was pastor. When we drove by him on the highway he would no longer even wave at us.

Two more years we stayed in DeWitt. During those years I began to feel lonely and ostracized. At that time I thought it was my fault, that I was, in the lingo of the day, simply a "square". Years later as I revisited my childhood in search of wisdom and healing I realized that my feelings might have been bigger than my own faults. Perhaps the fact that my family was subsequently labeled "nigger-lovers" was a factor I couldn't see back then.

Ron McDonald

I moved away from DeWitt as lonely as I had ever felt, anxious to start with a new peer group in another town.

The year after we left we heard that Mr. LaFargue came back to the church. Brother Thurston Masters was the new preacher, and we heard that someone brought up the same motion again, that colored people would not be seated if they came to the church. Brother Masters, we understood, did not feel the same way my father felt, did not oppose it, and it passed. (I found out nearly 40 years later that this story was not true. In fact, Mr. LaFargue never again was very active in the church, the re-vote never occurred, and Bro. Masters never did face the same issue Dad had stood up to. But I *thought* it was true for 40 years!)

I reacted to the news with bitterness and rage, for by that point in my life I understood what it meant. That rage lasted and lasted for years. I could remember the courage of my dad and that something significant had been planted in me with that event. I would live my life inclusively, living in mixed racial neighborhoods, enrolling my kids in inner-city schools, having friends of all races. But still, the rage and bitterness over that decision in our absence harbored inside of me for 20 years. Someone else hadn't had the courage to stand up for what I knew was right.

One day I was talking with my father about that experience in DeWitt, and he suddenly exclaimed, "O, Ron, I want to tell you something that happened to me in Little Rock the other day!

"I was in the city for a conference and Johnny Schallhorn came up to me. Do you remember him?"

"Yes, I do," I replied. "He took over the hardware store and was married to Lucree."

Home Again

Dad continued, "He said, 'Charles McDonald, I remember you so well. Do you remember me?' I said, 'Of course I do.' Then he said, 'I'm the mayor of DeWitt now, and I want to tell you something you've done for me and for us in DeWitt.'

"Johnny said, 'Years ago I was a segregationist like everyone else I knew. I never thought there was anything wrong with it. When all that controversy happened around seating blacks in our church, I kept hearing you raise questions that made me wonder if segregation was right. You made some sense to me. Do you know what? I'm the Mayor of DeWitt now, and we are having dialog between blacks and whites and doing some of the most progressive things in race relations ever done in DeWitt. I want to thank you for how you helped.'"

Forgiveness is not just an experience of releasing another person from guilt. It is also the experience of discovering that the judgmental and small-mindedness we've harbored for years is just as bad as the transgression that led to the outrage. That kind of forgiveness sometimes comes to us like a shattered glass. It came to me at that point. Twenty years of rage and bitterness shattered on the floor. I realized that somehow or another my faith had been so small that I didn't believe that some seeds would fall on good soil. For 20 years I had harbored and nurtured anger at folks in DeWitt as if God might not have been working miracles even through their transgressions. In spite of my narrow-minded rage, there were seeds from that time in DeWitt that had fallen on fertile soil and had grown and provided good fruit.

It wasn't just Johnny and DeWitt that was being transformed. I was, too. Johnny's story to Dad pulled up the weeds of my own outrage and freed me from the curse of self-righteousness.

No other story in my life has had such a dramatic effect upon me. In that small town I began to understand much more than church politics. I began to see the place of courage and conflict in the lives of people, and how there is a spirit that works through even the most bigoted people for eventual good. I saw much of this through a relationship that would be sustained even up to this point in my life — my relationship with my father. It has been a relationship that has drawn me deeper and deeper into life, for life and love are so intertwined.

Shortly after that event, Dad found a statement of openness that he printed on the weekly church bulletin. The statement invited all people to our church. It did not refer specifically to all races, but could have to the discerning person. When I returned to DeWitt 30 years later and saw the same statement still on the bulletin, I knew that it was a statement that had gotten inside of me. It was part of the attitude of openness that Dad taught and lived. It was an attitude that I eventually came to understand was rooted in the meaning of faith. Faith, I have come to see, is not a closed door. It is open. From that openness I have grown in my faith, which led me to take a trip with my father back through the churches he pastored, the churches that nurtured me through my childhood. This book is about that journey of faith.

Chapter Two

I'M NOT LIKE MY DAD

A large man with a large personality, Dad was the center of our family of nine. My mother, though smarter and a great influence herself, did not have the emotional power Dad carried with him. It was not negative emotional power. Dad was Mr. Fun and Caring to us. Mother worked quietly behind the scenes. Dad was out front letting us all know it was OK.

A United Methodist minister, he loved people, and they loved him.

Despite the courage I remember him displaying in DeWitt, he didn't really like conflict. He was a peacemaker who felt the stress of occasional conflict in his stomach. The grandson and nephew of Methodist ministers, he took their deep commitment to people, found his own way of spinning Southern Christian wisdom, and was successful in every church he served. I have little doubt that he could have followed his Uncle Paul Galloway and become a bishop had he been interested in the politics required and had the ambition necessary to achieve that position. Instead, he stayed rooted in the pastoral ministry that he so deeply loved.

Our whole family became such a part of the church that the place where we truly heard Dad express his love for us was in his deeply felt prayers, especially when he broke from prescribed prayers at Christmastime and Eastertime and thanked God with a quivering voice, full of emotion, of his love for his family, his wife, and his sons. For us, family and church were interwoven.

Ron McDonald

I wanted to be just like my dad until I had to confront the dark side of myself during my early 20s. That shocking revelation—that I was capable of meanness, rage, and even violence—sent me into an introspective journey that led me, surprisingly, right to Dad. Taking the magnifying glass of personal therapy and focusing it on my dad and his weaknesses, I saw a man so prone to avoidance of conflict that he had taught me how to suppress my feelings of anger until they were dangerously enraged. Dad, despite being one who would stand tall in situations where courage and strength were required, despite being fundamentally a peacemaker, was, I began to believe, afraid of his own rage. And that rage had become mine. So I vowed to be different. Sometimes abrasively, I rejected as much of my dad's shadow as I could. Accompanying that rejection was an illusion that he was not also part of the best of me.

Ironically, I was in seminary when I vowed to not be like my dad. I decided to turn away from my plan to become a United Methodist minister and become a writer. I would not hide from emotions like I perceived him to have done. I would be a more physical man, a more introverted man, a "better" man. In my hubris I was too angry at my father's shadow to see his light.

I was right in some ways. For every man, including my dad, has a shadow, and always a part of that shadow is not a conscious part of the self. Sometimes only a person close enough to see the inner person can truly identify the shadow and its destructive tendencies. I may have been full of hubris and judgment, but I did see the truth. He was a good man with feet of clay.

And I would not be like him!

Times were tough between us. We kept talking, but I mostly steered away from what I was feeling and thinking.

Home Again

I was too critical, and I had seen how hurtful those thoughts were the few times I did tell him how negatively I thought about him. I may have been angry, but I didn't really want to hurt him.

I tried to be a writer, moved to Connecticut, changed churches (and became a Quaker), married my present wife, Susan, and she became pregnant.

When my first son, Jonah, was born, I was bowled over with feelings. I wrote a song that expressed a new feeling for me:

> *I never knew I could love any baby*
> *As deeply as I love this new child of mine*
> *I never believed I could so love an infant*
> *'Til he nestled in my arms and looked into my eyes.*

Although I hadn't written the song yet, those were the feelings inside of me when I dialed the telephone to call Dad. I'll never forget that conversation. I still didn't want to be like my dad. I said to him, "Dad, I can't believe how much I love this baby. I didn't know it was possible to love so deeply. It must be coming from God, because I'm not capable of it."

Dad said to me, "Ron, that's exactly how I felt when you and your brothers were born."

I felt a gasp inside of myself, and almost dropped the phone. It was as if someone had slapped me and said, "You're just like your dad." In spite of myself I was just like him.

Six years later I went to a conference and heard a pastoral counselor, John Patton, speak about forgiveness. He said that we cannot willfully forgive another person. When we do that we're being self-righteous, condescending: "*I'll* forgive you." It doesn't feel right. He said that forgiveness happens to us when we finally recognize that we're just like the very person we've been trying to condemn.

At that conference I suddenly knew what had happened to me six years before in that conversation with my dad. In spite of my desire to not forgive, in spite of my self-righteousness in saying "I will not be like him," I had discovered that the man whom I would condemn was just like me, that I was just like him.

Forgiveness had happened to me against my own will.

Dad's and my relationship blossomed from there in ways I had previously resisted. I learned not only how deeply I loved him—and how deeply he loved me—but also how much I *liked* him! Perhaps my rebellion had been essential to this change, but I knew it was completed and I could meet my dad in a new, fully open way.

Still, old resolutions die hard. I didn't want to be a minister like him. Despite seminary training, despite six years of work as a campus minister, despite three years of clinical training in pastoral counseling, despite earning a Doctor of Ministry, despite two certifications as a pastoral counselor from the American Association of Pastoral Counselors, despite constant association with other ministers in "ministerial alliance" groups and "ministers support groups," I still hung onto the idea that, as a member of the Religious Society of Friends (Quakers), the church I had converted to at 27 years old, a church that does not ordain, I was *not* a minister, but a layperson in ministry. For some reason which I'm still only partially aware of, I did not really want to be a minister, and that notion wouldn't die easily.

One evening as I was walking outdoors and planning a sermon for a church where I was to be the guest preacher, I accidentally said to myself, "Admit it, Ron, you are a minister down to your bones." To borrow a phrase from a familiar denomination—John Wesley's words—I felt "strangely warmed." Once again I felt the liberation of letting go of an illusion that I am essentially different from Dad. No, I realized in relief, it's more true and liberating to know that we're more alike than unlike. I'm not my dad, but I'm just like my dad.

With that last conscious bit of resistance out of the way, my soul was free to imagine an idea. What if Dad and I were to travel back to all the churches of his ministry while I was growing up—five of them—and share a passing of the mantle of ministry from father to son with each of those five congregations? When I first got the idea I dropped it immediately, thinking that it was a stupid, narcissistic father-son bonding experience that only the men's movement would appreciate.

But it wouldn't let go. I kept having the fantasy of preaching a shared sermon in those five churches. I thought of it so often that I had to listen to myself. It felt like a spiritual journey I wanted to take.

I asked Dad if he might be interested in it, and he quickly said yes. Then I dropped it for five years.

It would take me those five years to finally begin this journey. By that time Dad was 70 years old, fully retired and already reflecting back on his ministerial experiences in a new way. He was ready to go.

This was a journey that would mean more to us both than we imagined.

Chapter Three

I HOPE THIS ISN'T JUST SOME FATHER-SON BONDING CRAP

Does anyone really know why we take pilgrimages? Where does the yearning come from? Why do we go to those special places? What makes them so special? Could it be that we are trying to heal a split within ourselves that can't be done any other way? Could it be that only in a journey are we truly seeking with body and soul that which has been missing?

I have taken lots of risks in my life, but they've mostly been for thrills. Every now and then, though, I feel compelled to take a risk that makes me quake inside. It might be an urge to speak out in public in a tense or a reverent situation. It might be accompanied by a decision made without a sense of certainty. Some risks have an aura of being spirit-led about them. They are a journey into the unknown.

I felt that kind of unease when I finally wrote to the pastor of Holly Grove, Arkansas, where I was born, asking if Dad and I could come and preach there. I felt it even more in February 1997 when he said yes. He called me and we set a date for April 29.

Already that spring had not been a typical one for me. I was working very hard towards major certification as a pastoral counselor. I was to meet a national committee in Phoenix in May to determine whether or not I would be certified as Diplomate in the American Association of Pastoral Counselors.

Home Again

I was nervous and preoccupied. Driving to my folk's home in Conway on April 28 I was wishing I hadn't set this up. Not only was I not sure what we were really doing, I felt unprepared. I knew what I would say in Holly Grove, but my doubts were nearly overwhelming.

I wanted to do it, but I didn't, too. Was this the beginning of a fantasy come true, a potentially meaningful experience, or was this just a father-son fling? Was it a sort of narcissistic "look how great we are" show? Or was it a real effort to understand and express something important? Was it for others or just ourselves? Would it be meaningful to the folks in Holly Grove?

We had been talking about it for a month, off and on. Unlike me, Dad had not been preoccupied with something else. This idea had captured his imagination. Once during a visit prior to the trip, as we stood outside of town stargazing at the Hale-Bopp Comet, he said to me, "I think this might be the closure of ministry for me." I saw tears in his eyes, and he added, "I've been thinking about your comment that this is a passing of the mantle of ministry. I think that *is* what this is about."

When I got to Conway the night of the 28th, we talked, Mother, Dad, and me. Holly Grove was, in fact, a very significant place for Mother, too, but she had her usual grace about letting this be just between Dad and me. She claimed she felt sickly with some diabetes related symptoms, but I knew those symptoms, although real and troublesome, were really a gracious reason to let us do this alone. We were nervous about it, not knowing fully what this was about or how we would do it. Our talk that night was merely about details on the order of worship. The main event was to be a shared sermon, Dad first, me second. Dad talked about his plan to speak about memories and the meaning of the cross in his ministry. He had written out his sermon. I had mine in my head—four short stories related to shame and forgiveness, and reconciliation.

We rose at 6 AM. Dad said he had not slept well but felt refreshed and ready. I knew this trip had kept him awake. He had spent his 40 days waiting for this experience, and last night he was like a child waiting on Christmas. I didn't have the same level of anticipation as he did. There was so much on my table that this seemed a little like another work day among many. We both felt nervous, but at least I didn't have to worry about embarrassing myself with forgetting somebody like he did. I had been an infant when we moved from Holly Grove. Holly Grove didn't mean that much to me, I didn't think. What bothered me about this was the still nagging suspicion that this trip might be a sort of selfish using of the people in Holly Grove for some "father-son bonding crap," as one of my brothers had jokingly referred to this trip.

It was a two hour drive, so we left around 6:30 AM. On the way we talked of our lives together. Both of us have such strong feelings for one another, full of respect and admiration. There's none of the competitiveness I used to have towards him, and none of the natural paternalism he used to convey toward me. Our relationship has really matured beyond father-raising-son to father-son as friends. We talked of the anticipated significance of this journey. "I've been thinking about this every day for a month," he told me. Although both of us were managing our nervousness well, we knew without speaking that we hadn't invited anyone in the family to come along because of our insecurity about this.

"I'm kind of glad Holly Grove is such a small church," I said.

"Me, too," replied Dad. "There won't be many there to embarrass ourselves in front of if this isn't such a good idea."

"Yeah," I said, "but I have a feeling that this is much greater than we are, that this isn't just about us."

"So do I," said Dad. He could have added, "That's another reason I'm nervous about it." But I understood that without him saying it.

Dad told me about Holly Grove as we got closer to it. He had moved there in 1949, straight out of seminary. His assignment to the Methodist Church was his first pastorate after graduating from Perkins Seminary in Dallas. Holly Grove was and is a town of around 800 people in the flat delta farmlands—smack in the middle of some of the richest soil in the world. For years it has been one of those football rich towns. The high school football team, despite its slim pickings, consistently out-performed itself. A little Class B school, I always noticed Holly Grove football teams were 8-2, 9-1, 10-0, year after year. Football, farming, and the church had been the centers of town life.

It was the place where Dad had first been confronted with racial injustice. Once he made reference in a sermon to "a colored lady." After church, one of the church leaders pulled him aside and said, "Charlie, don't ever refer to a colored woman as a lady."

"That bothered me a lot," Dad said. "Got me to thinking and seeing other things that bothered me.

"We had boardwalks next to the streets in town, and whenever a black person met a white person on it, he or she had to step off the boardwalk and let the white person pass by. I didn't like that, especially when it was wet and muddy, so whenever I could I would step off the boardwalk first and let the black person walk by.

Ron McDonald

"When I came into town I was driving a 1936 Ford car with an extra tire I'd picked up tied on the back. I had the feeling my junky looking car embarrassed some people. The preacher before me, Brother Campbell, had his own refrigerator and mattress, which he took with him when he moved. I didn't, however, so for the first few days I was virtually camping out in the parsonage! The church had to hurry up and get me a mattress and refrigerator.

"I was scared to death. This was my first church, and I had probably preached all of twelve times, so the people had to put up with me learning how to prepare and preach sermons.

"You know, Ron, this county, Monroe County is not just a part of our lives. It's part of our heritage. My grandfather, J. J. Galloway, back in 1937 or 1938 was pastor at Brinkley and later at Hughes — I remember the flood of 1937. Later, my uncle, Paul Galloway, was pastor at Clarendon. I've thought, isn't that something that the three of us were pastors of three of the communities in Monroe County."

We drove into town slowly. He kept pointing out places where he'd had various experiences. We drove past the church towards the downtown area. He said, "There's where I played tennis with J. B. Sain. J. B. died of cancer while I was here. He was a young man, and it was the first really difficult funeral I led — I learned how to deal with the death of not just a member of the church, but a friend.

"So many memories come back to me now.

"But I'm worried about remembering the people." He smiled and looked at me, "I've got half-timers, you know. That's when you can only remember names half the time."

"It may be Alzheimer's," I joked.

"Our family traditions were begun in this church. We had Uncle Paul [Galloway] come here and lead a youth

Home Again

activities week. The next year we had one of my favorite seminary professors, Dr. Wesley Davis, a New Testament professor, preach to us during Holy Week. He stayed at our house for the whole week.

"It was during the first Youth Activities Week we had here that I met Lois. She came here with the group she was working with from Brinkley. I told her she had to stop a recreational activity she was leading because it was time for worship. She got mad at me! But she still went out with me a bit later, and, of course, we married."

When we arrived at the church—a place I had only seen pictures of—two men were already there when we arrived: the minister, Charles Thompson, and Donnie Dearing. Donnie had been in high school when Dad was there. He was a farmer now, with a farmer's callused hands, a weathered face, and the down-to-earth gentleness of one who loved the land. Dad remembered him well. Charles was a heavy, clear-voiced man in his 50s who seemed articulate and intelligent. He had a look-you-in-the-eye availability. This church was one of two he pastored, the other one being in Clarendon about 15 miles away. The Clarendon church was the vital, strong church. Holly Grove was the secondary charge.

The church building was a well-preserved small sanctuary above a nice basement that served as the fellowship hall and classroom for children, and a small back area with a pastor's study and a very nice adult Sunday School classroom. We climbed the steps to the front door of the sanctuary, went inside and saw a beautiful room, simple with stained glass windows, a nice chancel area, and comfortable pews—seating for about 100-150. It was not in any disrepair. They took obvious pride in keeping the church building clean, well-decorated, and comfortable.

Ron McDonald

I set up my hammer dulcimer and took my guitar out of the case while a couple of persons arrived. Dad talked enthusiastically with them, and introduced me to them, telling me a short story about each person. After about the fifth person came in I had noticed two striking things. One was that each person he introduced me to had their family name on the stained glass windows. The other was the amount of recall of names and stories Dad was demonstrating. No one who entered was a stranger to him. This man who had just expressed his fear of not remembering was remembering everything.

It's not often an event like this happens—a former preacher returns with his son to share memories and reflections. Even though formal worship started at the appointed time of nine o'clock, it was clear to me from the start that this was special already, that worship had already begun. The people and Dad and I were already engaged in something unusual.

When formal worship began, I led most of the music with my hammer dulcimer and guitar. Dad and I both shared in the prayers, readings, and sermon. It was nice and the people were listening intently. For Dad and I it was particularly special.

Like most fathers, he told of his children with great pride before his sermon: "I want to tell you about my family. David was born here on November 3, 1950. Dr. Herb Stone was our doctor. He also delivered Ron. Dr. Stone's son has been my doctor in Conway beginning when I, unfortunately, had a mild stroke. He is a fine doctor." (We often joke with Dad that the best thing about his stroke is that, in having a CAT scan, we found out that he does have a brain.)

"David and his wife, Lou, and son, Scott, live in Conway near Lois and I. He is a counselor to the deaf in

Little Rock. Ron was born here on December 14, 1951. He has a wife, Susan, and two sons, Jonah and Jesse, and works as a pastoral counselor at the Church Health Center in Memphis, a ministry to the poor of the city. We moved to Ozark in 1952, where Don and Tom were born. Don is in his psychiatric residency in Memphis, is married with two daughters. Tom married a Japanese woman, Junko. They live in Conway also where he is an editor at the Log Cabin Democrat. They have two little girls. We moved to Pocahontas in 1958 where Jim was born. He administers a home health and hospice program in Fayetteville and lives with his wife and three children. Mark was born in 1966 in Rogers. He's a United Methodist minister in Huntsville, married with two children. David Driver became a part of our family while we lived in Rogers. We unofficially adopted him. He had grown up in the Arkansas Methodist Children's Home in Little Rock. He became a United Methodist minister as well, married, and had a daughter. Unfortunately, David passed away a few years ago. So we've had seven sons, and now have 11 grandchildren. We've been very fortunate."

Preaching has always been Dad's creative passion. He pours so much of himself into it. He spoke of the central symbol in his experience of ministry—the cross. Beginning with the time he stood over the city of Fayetteville next to the lighted cross on Mount Sequoia and felt called into ministry, to the many different crosses in the churches he served, to the crosses in our homes and even in his pocket, he shared with the congregation how rich this Christian symbol has been for him.

Storytelling is my creative emotional outlet. I told stories about our lives together as I grew up, as we grew apart, and as we grew back together—the story of my discovery of my commonness with him just when I was trying hard not to be like him. I ended my part of the sermon by singing "Jonah's Song" — the song I wrote about my deep spiritual awakening at the birth of my first son. Many in the congregation were wiping their eyes. Dad was; I was, too.

After worship we adjourned to the adult Sunday School class together. Rev. Thompson left for Clarendon, while most of the congregation stayed. The teacher, an elderly woman who bantered with Dad over some old memories, began the class by saying, "I'm not teaching a class today. We're just going to keep talking." Bantering and remembering continued for a while

Dad told stories of their lives together from his pastoral perspective. It was like he was telling them who they had been, even who they are now. "This was a simple town back then in many ways, a place where you could teach a young preacher like me how to pastor. We had many young people that I used to do a lot with. We would pick up a whole bus load and bring them here. We really reached out into the community. I used to visit the school a lot, particularly during football season. This was a thriving church."

Donnie asked me about my counseling work. I told them, "I work at a health care clinic for the working poor, for folks who cannot afford health insurance. It's called the Church Health Center. We are trying to reclaim the church's biblical and historical commitment to care for the poor who are sick. My job there is pastoral counselor. We find that maybe 50 percent of the patients who come to see our primary care physicians are not suffering from a medical problem as much as a spiritual or psychological problem. Those people are referred to me.

"For example, I saw a woman recently who came to the doctor complaining about heart problems. The doctors

Home Again

found nothing, but upon asking her if she was under much stress she confessed that she was very upset at work. They referred her to me and she told me that she was being criticized constantly at work and at home by her angry husband. Instead of focusing on her physical heart, we found that the most important task was to help her with a sad heart, to help her gain the confidence and courage — the heart — to stand up for herself and change her situation."

I changed the subject back to them: "I honestly believe that churches and towns like yours are a big part of the hope for our future. People everywhere are learning that the urban life is so complex and insecure, and that we need to look at the simplicity offered in rural towns. In the small towns I grew up in, professional pastoral counselors like me were unnecessary because of the presence of community healers. These were the people who had wisdom and were trusted to keep secrets. You knew who those persons were." They all nodded as I talked. "You would have known who to go to with problems, who would have listened well, offered good advice, and kept it confidential. Pastoral counselors like me are in business to a great extent because the community healers are mostly hidden now, and the problems people deal with are more complicated. The problems are virtually the same, but the complexity of our culture makes it so much more difficult to find solutions. We pastoral counselors are just doing what the historic church did through its wisest, best people."

The meeting shifted back and forth between Dad's reminiscing and my talking about what was happening in our world today and what I, as a representative of the church, was seeking to do about it.

I began to sense that they were depressed. I asked them, "Is your church, are *you*, discouraged?" To a person, they all quietly nodded. One man spoke: "To be honest, we are having trouble financially. We can't pay our conference apportionment. We keep up the church building, but it's hard."

I asked them about the town. They told us the typical southern town story of decline and shift in racial percentages. When Dad was there 50% of the people were white, 50% black. Now, they said, it's 85% black. One person added, "There are serious drug problems now. We even have to lock our doors, even when we're home." They told of the high school turning all black. The white children have been sent to private schools.

I've heard these stories before, but this time the stories of the breakdown of the old Southern culture, rooted in segregation, were not bitter stories. To my surprise there was a willingness to admit their confusion and desire for better relationships. One woman said, "I was the town Mayor, and when I retired, the next Mayor was black." She spoke with pride about her role in the town, and with surprising acceptance of the shift of power. One man said that he thought blacks and whites need one another. He talked of a partnership that, despite there being a power imbalance, was to be built on mutual respect.

I remember speaking at a church in Hughes, Arkansas, a town about 50 miles from Holly Grove. Afterwards we spoke of racial relationships. I told them that I thought reconciliation was possible and had experienced some significant positive changes in my life in Memphis. One of the men said to me, "It's not the same here in Arkansas. You'd have to live here to understand." Of course, I had grown up in these delta towns. I knew he was not open to reconciliation. Prejudice is a serious illness.

Home Again

I did not sense such animosity in this church in Holly Grove. I knew it was present at some level, but they spoke of occasional interracial worship, saying, "No one walked out when the blacks came in. Plenty of people would have left some years ago." They actually spoke with pride about their strides away from prejudice. Although I knew the economic structures still gave power to the white landowners, a fact that kept blacks handicapped with limited vision and angry discouragement, it gave me hope to hear this desire to grow beyond the bonds of prejudice. These men and women were not espousing that old "I may be prejudiced, but there's a good reason for it," that has so dominated the white South. Instead, they were saying, "We're trying, but it's hard." Perhaps someday the economic power imbalances will shift—they have politically. I was hearing of an attitude shift, which may be setting the table for deeper means of reconciliation.

Sunday School time was up. We adjourned for an hour while folks went to get their covered dishes and Dad and I would take a walk through the town streets. When we stepped outside, Barner Richardson was with us, saying he was going to walk with us. He took us on a history tour of the town. Downtown buildings were, as he said, "bombed-out"—crumbling or in need of repair. Not all, of course, but on one side of the street nothing substantial was still open. It was another testament to the crumbling of the old Southern structures.

Segregation was at its root an economic system. Without segregation the town's economic structure was in disrepair, and nothing just and civil had yet replaced it. It's true that the only large legitimate business owned by blacks is the church. The other big business is drugs, and that is destructive recreation. Someday I hope whites wake up to the need to offer jobs with excellent pay and benefits for black laborers—jobs with hope and dreams built in. When that happens, whites might not be able to maintain such a high standard of living, but their lives will be surrounded by happy people, people who can be friends and colleagues instead of politely suspicious outsiders. It will take some courage, because when one white owner raises wages, most other white owners will pressure him or her not to disturb the market for everybody else. I pray that folks in a church like Holly Grove will join together and make such a change, so that the church is a place of courageous folks, not just a place where one courageous individual is surrounded by lip service from his or her friends.

Barner told us of the recent mayor's use of federal funds for herself. He showed us a beautiful old house a block from main street. "Our mayor, a black woman, got a federal grant to remodel the house for a day care center, then six months after the remodeling she moved the day care center to another building on the edge of town and moved herself into this house—remodeled at government expense. It didn't help race relations, although I think the blacks were as upset about it as the whites. But I guess white politicians have done that kind of things for years—maybe just a little less obviously."

Dad told of the train that used to come through town just in back of the parsonage where we lived. Now the tracks are gone, replaced by a beautiful greenway (surrounded by shabby businesses). He said that my brother, David, and I were afraid of trains, so he used to take us outside when a train came by and hold us while it passed. Suddenly I knew why I have always—in my conscious memory—loved trains. Somewhere in my preconscious memory has been the warmth of being held in my daddy's arms associated with trains.

Home Again

We went back to the church for a pot luck dinner. Dad and I were served first, and as we sat down, I said to Dad, "This is fun!"

"Yes, it is," he replied.

Donnie's wife, sitting next to me, said, "When I graduated from high school I couldn't decide if I wanted to go on to college or do something else. Finally my mother suggested I talk with your Dad. She said he had just left the educational world and might give me some suggestions or something. I did, and after a couple of hours of talking, he suggested that I consider studying education. He said, 'As a teacher you'll have a skill that you can set aside for a while, then go back to when you're ready, and it's usable everywhere.' I thought that was a great idea, and I became a teacher. I've taught for 30 years."

As we were leaving Donnie pulled me aside and said, "Your dad meant an awful lot to me."

We got into the car, and as we drove off Dad said, "Ron, this was the greatest day of my life." Then he added, "If I were to die and go to heaven tomorrow, I would say to God, 'I was in heaven yesterday.'"

Two days later I flew to Arizona for a conference. On the plane ride I watched "The Preacher's Wife," a movie about a preacher and his wife seeking to save a church. It's a tear-jerker movie, much like "It's a Wonderful Life." I found myself weeping, and I knew that my tears were not just about the movie. I had been passed the mantle of ministry from my father, a very noble and important calling. It wasn't just about me and Dad, though. We were doing something about what needs to happen from one generation to the next—a gracious, definitive blessing that says, "You do the work now, because it is right that you carry on and make the world a better place to live." I also knew why Dad was so moved by the experience. He knew that his ministerial efforts were being sustained through the lives of people he had nurtured. That's why he felt this was his first day in heaven, for it was new life—eternal life. He had spoken of the cross. Those who carried on had represented resurrection.

God, what a blessing!

The plane I was on was taking me to Phoenix, Arizona, where I was to "meet the committee" to determine my capability of functioning as a leader and teacher in the pastoral counseling movement. Arriving in Phoenix in the early afternoon, I took to the public trails to relax, meditate, and enjoy the desert. The next morning I rose early, dressed neatly, and waited my turn to meet with the committee members.

The meeting began with difficulty. I was sharing with them a tape recording and write-up of a supervisory session I had led with a trainee, and one of the men quickly questioned the wisdom of a comment I had made to my supervisee, and others agreed with him. I felt defensive, they were trying hard to be kind, diluting their criticism. Confusion set in, and I was quite worried that I was "failing" the interview. The best I could do was to say, "I'm not sure what is happening right now. Would you explain yourselves to me again, and I'll try to listen better." Immediately the tension lessened, they spoke clearly, I heard them, and we began to discuss a common issue supervisors encounter. The committee of three confronting one became a committee of four discussing our work as supervisors.

After a while they wanted to know more about me, not just my work. I told them, with tears, of the experience Dad and I had just had. One of the men wept as well as it touched feelings of his own related to his father. The pass/fail vote that they had an hour and a half later was immaterial. We had become colleagues. I passed 3-0.

I was pretty happy! That night I walked into the annual banquet hall, sat down at a table next to some friends, one who was one of the committee members. Just before the blessing was to be shared, a host rose, welcomed us, and announced that there was a door prize. She asked us to look under the chair we were seated at. Under my chair was a index card labeled, "Grand Prize." I lifted it up, and she invited me to the front where I was awarded a green stained glass Thunderbird.

Now I have always liked eagles. I've danced like a eagle in interpretative dance classes, memorized poems about eagles, driven distances to see bald eagles. I've also loved Native American art. It lifts me up towards my Cherokee and Creek heritage. And my office is dark green. This Thunderbird was not only the Native American representation of the eagle, it was not only dark green, it was exactly what I would have picked out on my own in any gallery! Wow!

It didn't stop there. The next day I went on a hike to the top of a nearby mountain with a friend who shared with me moments of deep intimacy, a truly inspiring hike and conversation.

After the conference I drove to Williams, Arizona, a gateway village to the Grand Canyon, and began eating some very good food at a Mexican restaurant. A guitar player and singer sat down and began to play for us. I am a guitar player, too, and I have a large repertoire of songs that I enjoy singing. For an hour this musician played songs from MY repertoire! I had trouble eating, for it was hard to sing and eat at the same time.

I left Williams early the next morning for the Grand Canyon. It was about 45 minutes later than I had planned to leave, for I wanted to get to Mather Point in time for sunrise. I watched the sky getting brighter and brighter, finally resigning myself to missing sunrise. I drove up to the entry gate, and after sitting there, honking, and finding no one, I drove on through—free. Stopping at Mather Point, I stepped onto the overhanging rock just before sunrise. There was a crowd of about 200 folks waiting for the event in utter silence. Together we watched as the sun rose in the east, changing the colors of the Grand Canyon over and over again. It was spectacular.

Around 7 am I hit the Bright Angel Trail and hiked the top part of the inner canyon and back up the Kaibab Trail by late afternoon—one of those exhausting, exhilarating hikes that happens but a few times in a life-time.

Back to Williams, I slept soundly that night, then drove down the Sedona Canyon highway, stopping at Slide Rock State Park. As I walked along the rock river bed with the rushing waters of the winter, I felt that I had been blessed with far more than one should receive in one week. Every experience I had had that week was a peak experience! I started wondering what it meant. Did God have some special plan for me?

I stepped into the river water, feeling an urge to be washed by the cool waters. Taking off my shoes, I wadded in, but the water was not just cool. It was so cold my feet hurt. I couldn't stand the feel of the pebbles on my feet. I wished I had brought along my river sandals, but, since I hadn't, I resigned myself to just walking alongside the water. Then, jumping onto a rock in the middle of the river where I would gather myself and jump on across to the other side, I stopped, looked down, and there was an abandoned pair of river sandals! No one was nearby, it was Monday, they were mostly worn out, so I knew someone had left them on Sunday and wouldn't return for them. They were mine for the wading! I put them on and they fit! I waded in the water to my heart's content.

By now I was exclaiming out loud, "OK, God, I'm listening! You've got my attention!"

I returned home a changed man. Despite having no clear idea of what I was being called to, I was more open than before. And like Quakers often say and I believe, "the way will open; we must only sit quietly and wait."

Maybe that's what a pilgrimage is about—it's a quest for change. It's an open way, and what's beyond the opening is a radical transformation of self.

Chapter Four

OZARK

Ozark, Arkansas, is a mountain town of 1600 people one hour from Ft. Smith. We lived in Ozark for six years beginning in 1952. It is where my memories begin. It is where my parents made some of their best life-long friends. Ozark, like Holly Grove, is still a small town, but unlike Holly Grove, where farming is so obviously the key to economic life, it is one of those towns surrounded by half successful farms and small commercial businesses. Look at Holly Grove and you *know* why it exists. It's a center of a rich farm culture in some incredibly fertile land. Look at Ozark and you *wonder* why it exists. Ozark was more of a gathering place for diverse, rural people. The Methodist Church was a block from the square on Route 64, the main road through town. Just west of the church Arkansas Highway 23 turns south and crosses the Arkansas River. Below the bridge was the town dump, a beach. Every day debris and garbage was dumped on the river beach, to be bulldozed into the river every afternoon, swept away. Out of sight, out of mind. Thus, the river was but a sewage ditch, not a play place, not a natural blessing. It would be years until people were to see the results of this vicious indifference to nature and begin to see the river as a beautiful place, not as a tool.

We moved to Ozark when I was six months old. We lived there six years. Two of my six brothers were born in Ozark, Don and Tom. My earliest memories are of the house and backyard. I still remember telling my mother, "Mother, David and I are making mud pies and Donnie is eating them." And I remember the switch that Mother used to punish David, Don, and me. We used to set David up as a look-out, Donnie holding the chair that I would climb onto, reaching to the top of the refrigerator where the switch was kept. Quietly, secretly, I would break it into pieces, put it back down where it was, then we'd run. We thought Mother would never know what happened to it!

Most of my memories of Dad in Ozark are of him as young and physically energetic. He was in his late 20s and early 30s—his physical prime—and I remember him running behind our bikes as we learned to ride, walking tall, always carrying someone, mowing the lawn, helping to maintain the church and parsonage. They were the days when he was learning how to be a father. By the time we left Ozark, he had four children, all boys, and a wife who was tired, often overwhelmed, and, as I remember her, often grouchy. Except when adults were around. Then Mother was full of life, smiling, and obviously happy to be engaged in the adult world that we usually kept her from.

July 4, 1997

My family and I are in Conway on a vacation trip. Dad and I were talking about our next trip, to Ozark. Dad told me that he's planning to preach about Jesus' and Peter's interaction at the end of John when Jesus tells him to "tend my lambs, feed my sheep, care for my sheep." He said Father Galloway, his grandfather and the first Methodist preacher in the family, advised him to remember those words in his ministry. Father Galloway's last sermon was preached in Ozark when we were there.

Dad kept telling me how he would make three points in his sermon in Ozark. I interrupted with a smile, "You can't think of anything without it having three points, can you?"

He laughed and said, "That's the way I was taught. You make the point, illustrate the point, then tell 'em what to do with it."

July 5, 1997

The next morning Dad was sick. Not just sick, seriously sick. Mother calmly informed us that she was taking him to the hospital. We met them later in the emergency room. He was being admitted with internal bleeding. As he left for the hospital room with Mother, he said, "Put on my tombstone, 'See, I told you my side was hurting.'" Later, when I went with my brother, David, to visit him, he was in good spirits, trusting the medical care he was receiving. We talked about our hope that he and I could still go to Ozark next week, but knew we might have to postpone it.

As I was leaving to go back to Memphis, I reached out, touched Dad's hand, and said goodbye. His cheerful demeanor suddenly vanished and I saw eyes filled with fear and worry. It was just a moment, but now I knew that his courage isn't without work and struggle.

July 11, 1997

A week later I was back in Conway. Dad had recovered quickly and decided he wanted to go. We were both nervous for different reasons. I wasn't sure what I wanted to say. The story I wanted to tell was one that I felt might upset the pastor there, Rev. Roger Glover. Ever since contacting him I had had an intuition that he was reluctant to have us in his church, and when I told Dad of my feeling he told me that he and Roger had found themselves far apart theologically from time to time. Dad had been his District Superintendent in the early 70s, helping Roger

Home Again

enter seminary, but their theological orientations had never converged. Roger, Dad said, had particularly strong opinions against gays and abortion, issues Dad had differed with him over. So as I imagined telling "The Baalshentov's Servant", a story in which Christians are portrayed as pretty evil at one point, I wondered if Roger might be insulted by it. Perhaps our theologies were far apart. I hoped the differences between us—if there truly were differences—weren't too great to find reconciliation.

Whatever his theology, Roger called Dad nearly every day he was in the hospital. That said a lot about his character, and must say something important about his theology, too.

Dad was worried because he was afraid it might be a let-down from Holly Grove.

Mother was going with us this time, and Dad and I were both glad to have her along to share the experience with us.

July 12, 1997

We rose and left early Sunday morning, arriving in Ozark at 8:30 AM. As we drove through the town Dad and I remembered this place and that, but Mother kept saying, "I don't remember that," adding, "I guess I was always at home." I thought that's why Mother was, in my memory, grouchy so often. She didn't have a life! I once was pretty judgmental about that. Until I had children. Now I know!

At nine we picked up Roger, and after a few pleasantries, left for Cecil, the small church he pastors along with Ozark, where he had also asked us to preach. He spent most of the drive talking about his ministry in Ozark and Cecil. He asked me if I had planned a children's sermon, and although I hadn't, I told him I'd love to do it.

Ron McDonald

That meant I had to decide what story to tell on the drive to Cecil, which was hard to do with Roger sharing so much. I suppose I wasn't a great listener.

Cecil is a lovely white clapboard church with a clean, cozy sanctuary. The people were informal and quite friendly. I set up my dulcimer, then chatted with a few folks until time to start playing.

Roger began with a call to worship, introduced Dad and me, although he obviously couldn't remember my name and introduced me as "Charles' son."

I rose and spoke.

"My name is Ronald McDonald. I had that name first. My parents were playing a big joke on me. I've had to put up with a lot! Actually, they didn't know what they were condemning me to, but if they had've they'd have probably done it anyway. I've sometimes even gotten free hamburgers at McDonald's. When I do that, however, I have to put up with everybody looking at me while I eat. At least I don't have red hair. I'm glad I don't have red hair, although I'm starting to lose what I have. Still, I've got more than Dad."

The experience I had had in Holly Grove and Arizona had led me to talk about finding God's call. I told an old folktale for the children and others who appreciate the wisdom in children's stories.

> There once was a young a spider who wondered what would be his calling. He fretted over it often, only to be comforted by his mother, who would say, "Someday you will find that God has a special task for you. Keep learning to spin a web quickly and well, and the day will come when your gifts will be used for much good." They lived at the entrance of a cave in the land of Judea.

Home Again

Now in those days King Saul was chasing the young David throughout the countryside, afraid that David was seeking to usurp his throne. David, however, wasn't. He had no desire to take the throne he believed was granted to Saul by the Lord God. He would not usurp Saul's authority, so he simply kept running from Saul's intended fight. David knew that were he and his men to have to fight Saul, Saul might be killed. Carefully and stealthily, David avoided Saul's army.

One day when David found himself and his men closely pursued by King Saul and his army, they came upon the very cave that the young spider and his family lived in. David and his men broke through the spider webbing and hid in the cave.

As the spiders listen to the whispers of David and his men, they became aware of the nobility of David. Suddenly the little spider realized that if Saul's army came upon the cave and found the spider webs broken, they could guess that David was hiding in the cave and would be able to easily defeat, even kill, David and his men.

Quickly, the little spider went to work weaving a web across the entrance of the cave. His many months of practice made him skillful and quick. Just before King Saul and his army arrived at the cave, the little spider finished weaving a great web.

Saul's and his army's eyes widened when they at once realized that David and his men would almost certainly be holed up in the cave. They thought they had them at last, but when the first scouts set forth into the cave, they found before them the little spider's great web.

The leader exclaimed, "They cannot be here, for there is a great web across the entrance here. If they were here, they would have broken this web."

Turning away, the men and King Saul were amazed at the miraculous escape of David and his men.

"And that," I finished, "is how a little spider saved the young David, who would someday become King of Israel. For no matter how small our gift, God's call awaits. Sometimes even the smallest gift is used for the greatest purpose."

Inherent in this simple story was an expression of my hope that my simple gifts will be used for some purpose, as well as my sense of awe that had accompanied the first stage of this pilgrimage. Here I was home again with my Dad, soaking in the blessing only a father can bestow upon his son, seeking the call that was so deeply connected to my relationship to him. Dad was like a benevolent King Saul to me, and he was like the little spider, weaving his protective web before me so that I could receive the mantle of ministry from him.

Dad's prayer and sermon was an expression of his hope and the conviction that he had done his best. He said, "I began my ministry back in 1949 and received my first appointment in Holly Grove. My grandfather, J. J. Galloway, a Methodist minister who served in Arkansas for 40 years, while sitting on a front porch, said to me, 'Charles, you're starting your first church. I want to give you a little bit of advice. First, remember to save all you can and give all you can. John Wesley said for us to save 10%, and he also said to give 10%. Second, do you remember the passage where Jesus was talking to Simon Peter and asked him if he loved him?'

Home Again

"'Why, sure,' I said. 'I've studied it, and heard it preached on many times.'

"He then said, 'Jesus said, "Care for my lambs, tend my sheep, and feed my sheep." Charles, you must remember to be a pastor to people, care for the little children, and proclaim the word of God. That's what Jesus was really saying to Simon Peter.'

"Since then that's what I've sought to do in my ministry: be a pastor, care for children, and preach the word of God, seeking to lead people to the cross. My grandfather said, 'Charles, you remember that if you love people you can lead them to the cross—you lead them with love.'"

Despite the fact that this church was not a former home church for us, we could see that the people were deeply moved as he and I spoke. There was something archetypal, something universal about what we were doing. When a father and a son are able to share a common vision, common leadership, and common respect, especially when it is lighthearted and fun, it is a deeply worshipful experience. It was for Dad and I, and it was clearly for the people at Cecil.

After worship, as I walked to our car with Mother beside me, I said, "There's a real magic to this, isn't there, Mother?" She exclaimed, "There really is!"

A curious thing happened between Cecil and Ozark. Part of what I talked about was how I had avoided ministry and stayed away from Arkansas because I didn't want to be known just as my father's son. Roger had introduced us as "Charles and his son," not Charles and Ron. But in Ozark a half hour later, Roger introduced me, too. I suppose my part of the sermon had elevated me from Charles' son to Ron. There really is some truth to the idea that the son of a successful parent has to prove himself before he can be seen for what *he* is, and not just as an appendage of a parent.

Dad's sermon was like the one at Cecil, but he was able to add many of the stories of our time in Ozark. Particularly funny to me was his comment about how his mother had died with actual calluses on her knees from praying, but that his calluses were actually from laying the tiles on the floor of the educational building in Ozark. I interrupted him to say, "You mean those calluses of yours are not from prayer like you've been telling us?" He quipped, "I was praying that we would finish the job."

He also told of Father Galloway's influence on him, and of his last sermon in Ozark. I can hardly put into words the awesomeness of knowing that four generations later I'm walking the walk begun by my great grandfather, passed on to his son, my Uncle Paul Galloway, passed on to his grandson, my dad, and now on to me. It is truly a noble calling, even if I have resisted it for years.

My talk was once again about my struggle to accept my own calling to ministry. I had fun talking about the stories of my misbehavior in church. I said, "I'm fairly sure I would have been diagnosed ADHD—Attention Deficit Hyperactivity Disorder. They probably would have prescribed Ritalin for me. But my mother had another method—the switch." I told of our attempts to foil the switch's power by climbing up onto the refrigerator where the switch was kept. There we would break it to pieces, then, just so we wouldn't get into trouble, leave the pieces on top of the 'fridge where the switch had been. Mother suddenly spoke up and said, "I used to watch you boys do that and smile."

Home Again

Then I began to tell the story of the Baalshentov's Servant*:

There once was a wise Hasidic Jew named the Baalshentov. He would travel through the Roman Empire ministering to people and telling stories that brought out the best in all. He had a servant who always did whatever he asked of him.

When the Baalshentov was on his deathbed, he called before him his favorite people and relatives. The last before him was his faithful servant, who was, despite his sadness, excited about the possibility of receiving some great gift that would make his life easier. The Baalshentov said to the servant, "To you I wish to give my greatest treasure." At that the servant's heart leapt with joy—finally he would get a break! 'I give to you all of my stories and ask that you travel about and share them with whomever will listen.'

The servant, who always did whatever the Baalshentov requested, consented, but no sooner had he stepped away from his master, he was cursing this gift. "Of all the things he had to give me," thought the servant, "why *this*? Now I'll have to travel about begging for food, telling those stupid stories. What rotten fortune!"

He always did what the Baalshentov asked, though, so he traveled about and half-heartedly told the Baalshentov's stories.

One day he happened to hear that a wealthy man in Rome was offering a gold coin to anyone who could tell him one of the Baalshentov's stories he hadn't

---

* I heard this story from Professor Beldon Lane of Eden Theological Seminary. This is how I tell it.

heard. His heart leapt again, for he knew them all! This could be his break. He immediately set off for Rome and found the home of the man.

Arranging a meeting with him, he, at the appointed time, entered the man's house. The man said, "Welcome. I understand you can tell me many of the Baalshentov's stories. If I have not heard the one you tell me, I will give you a gold coin."

Smiling, the servant said, "I know them all. I'll tell you one." Then, as if a wind had blown away his memory, he could not think of one story. Flustered, he admitted his memory lapse. The man encouraged him to relax, but the servant could not jog his memory. Finally, he left in great frustration.

No sooner had he lay down that night than all the stories came back to him.

The next day he returned to the man's home, but just like the day before, when he began to tell a story, his memory failed him. Doubly frustrated, he left again.

That night, however, all the stories came back to him as before.

So he returned to the man again. Humbled now, with stories in mind, he began to speak when, for the third time, his memory failed him. "This is not right!" he exclaimed. "I know all the stories. I remember them at night but cannot remember them in your home! I am sorry, but I cannot stay here. I must go."

The man asked him to stay as he stepped to the door, and the servant stopped to apologize once more, then said, "Forgive me, but I am not lying. I *do* know the Baalshentov's stories. I was his servant. At least I can tell you one experience we had together that no

Home Again

one but me can tell. Then you will at least know that I am not an imposter.

"Once when we were in Turkey the Baalshentov came to me and told me that we were to travel to a particular village where he had some business to attend to. The village we were to go to was not a friendly village to Jews. In that village at this particular time of the year, the time of Easter, Christians would capture a Jew and crucify him to avenge what they said was our sin for the crucifixion of Jesus.

"But I always did whatever the Baalshentov asked. I collected the appropriate provisions, gathered animals to ride upon, and we traveled to the village. Into the Jewish section we entered, and the Baalshentov stopped at a home that, like all the others, was locked with shades drawn. He began to pound on the door. After some time a person opened the door who obviously recognized the Baalshentov, angrily saying, 'Don't you know what danger you are putting us in, making such a racket at this time of the year?!' They quickly pulled us into the house out of sight.

"Yet the Baalshentov went straight to the front window and opened the curtain wide. There before us was an angry mob of Christians coming to capture their Jew for their revenge. People in the house were trying to close the curtain when the Baalshentov said to me, 'Do you see that bishop leading the people?'

"There was a bishop dressed in his most sacred clothes leading the mob towards our house. 'Go to him right now and tell him the Baalshentov wishes to speak with him. Then bring him here.'

"I always did what the Baalshentov asked, but this time I thought I was going to my death. I left the house, walked up to the angry mob, and spoke directly to the Bishop. 'The Baalshentov wishes to speak with you. Please come with me.' To my utter amazement, the Bishop turned to the crowd and said, 'I must speak with this man. Go home, all of you. Go home.' The crowd of people, stunned and confused, stood there as the Bishop turned to me and said, 'Take me to him.' As we walked away, I could feel the mob dispersing and wandering away.

"I took the bishop to the house and he and the Baalshentov went into a back room and talked. All we could hear was their muffled voices. They spoke for three hours, and when they came from that back room, we could see that the bishop had been weeping. They embraced, and the bishop left, and the Baalshentov said to me, 'We can depart now.'"

At that moment the servant's head slumped downward. In an embarrassed voice he said, "I'm sorry. It's not really a story, but at least it will let you know that I was truly the Baalshentov's servant." He raised his head and saw that the man before him was weeping deeply. The servant said, "Please accept my apologies. I had no intention to offend you or hurt you. I am deeply sorry."

The man, however, held his hand forward in gratitude. "No," he said, "you don't know what good you have done for me.

"You see," he continued, "I was that bishop.

"Years ago I was a Jew like you — and a good Jew. But the persecutions frightened me so much that I converted to Christianity. I became a good Christian, so good, in fact, that I was appointed bishop. And even though I knew it was wrong, I went along with the crucifixion of the Jew every Easter. Then before you came to my village I had had a terrible series of dreams

Home Again

in which I was confined to hell for all of eternity. I was very disturbed, unable to determine the true state of my soul—except that I knew I was doing something very wrong. These dreams so convicted me that when you told me that the Baalshentov wanted to speak with me, I knew that God wanted to speak with me through him. I had to speak with him.

"In that back room I poured out my soul to him, and at the end of three hours of confession, tears, and anguish, he put his hand upon my knee and said, 'I think there is still hope for you. Go and end these persecutions, be a good man, and someday someone will come to you and tell you your own story. When that happens, when you hear your own story, you'll know that you have been forgiven.'

"When you were unable to remember any of the stories, something deep in me knew that the Baalshentov was in heaven arguing with God for my forgiveness. And now that you have told me my own story, I know that I am forgiven!"

When I came to this climatic statement I stopped, despite wanting to share further reflections on this powerful story. For there was an intrusive presence in the worship at Ozark—television. The local TV station broadcast the service. That meant that we had to start and end the service exactly on time. I found that to be a serious problem. As I told the story, finding the congregation deeply engaged in it—mesmerized—I naturally slowed my pace, embellished it, and watched the clock before me move steadily towards the 11:55 deadline. The congregation was leaning towards me, hanging on every word. The story had a life of its own, telling itself, even being transformed, just as I and the listeners were being moved to different places in the telling. Yet I had been charged with watching the clock. It was disconcerting enough that I was unable to interpret the story in the manner I really wanted to. Had I the time or a strategy for dealing with the clock's imposition on the leadings of the Spirit, I would have shared what the story has meant to me.

When I first heard the story and began telling it, it helped me accept the forgiveness I need towards those whom I often condemn. I identify with the bishop, disturbed by my complicity with what is wrong, seeking to feel peace within my own soul. I, too, am seeking a new understanding of my own story, an understanding that includes redemption and forgiveness. I also identify with the servant, especially right now, for he was a man struggling with his call. He had been called to share stories that were life-giving and healing, but, caught up in his desire for "early retirement" he was just doing his job. It wasn't a truly sacred calling. He was stuck with a gift that he didn't want to give. It is easy for me to imagine the transformation the bishop must have felt upon hearing the story.

I can hardly imagine, however, the impact of this experience on the servant. There he was seeking wealth, unable to use the very gifts he had been feeling cursed with, wallowing in despair. Then, despite his separation from the grace of God, he found himself the instrument of God's grace for someone else. God used him in spite of his sin. He must have been stunned. What an event this must have been in his life!

In my life I have been used a few times for the good of someone else, and as often as not, it has been despite my foul mood or inattention. It seems to me that God uses us for good despite ourselves.

Home Again

I could not share my full reflections on the story, for time was up. I kept thinking that this phenomenon does not let the Spirit run free. I couldn't help but think that this kind of interference with the spiritual life rarely happens in the African American church. There, if a preacher "gets the Spirit", he or she can keep on keeping on until the full message is shared. Because I had to be so clock conscious, I had to short-change the congregation on the full essence of the message. This is one of the basic problems with European-American worship. We have simply become too time conscious. I know we have schedules and obligations, but there are times when the Spirit moves and needs time to blossom. The Spirit needs flexibility.

On the other hand, had I not used some time to be funny and talk about myself as a hyperactive kid, maybe I could have given the Spirit more room. It's not all TV, but TV is definitely part of it. When you get right down to it, half of what hinders the movement of the Spirit is our narcissism. I might have wasted time indulging myself in narcissistically talking about my childhood in Ozark, while the church narcissistically wants to show off on TV. We're all guilty. We're all trying to do right. But I know that in this case the television structure kept some of the movement of the Spirit in a box.

The service ended shortly after I led the congregation in "Amazing Grace" with my dulcimer. Dad, Roger, Mother, and I then walked to the back of the church where my Mother embraced me with a wonderful hug. It's not like her to be so demonstrative with her affection, so I was quite touched by it. She had obviously been moved by the service and what I had said. It made me doubly glad she had come this time.

As we stood in line greeting people, Mother was the first to greet them. Thus, many shared their mutual stories with her as I, standing next to her, listened. It was such a contrast from the roles Dad and Mother had shared in years past. Dad had almost always been the first to receive the stories and greetings. He was the out-going one, the one with the most energy and wit. Mother, though, has grown into the one now who has the most energy, vitality, and might even be the most outgoing.

Years ago when I was in seminary my Mother came to visit me in New York City. Up until then I had seen her as a housewife and mother, period. While visiting me, however, she went to some classes, to plays, sightseeing and sharing talents, skills, and ideas that surprised me. I remember saying to myself, "This talented, intelligent person is my *mother*?" It was a nice discovery.

Déjà vu! This was my *mother* acting so gracious, outgoing, and alive! I think I was as proud of her as she was of me.

Another curious thing happened after worship. Roger had not set up a pot luck lunch for various reasons, so he and his wife took us out to eat at a local restaurant where some of his parishioners often ate after church. We sat at a long table, but the five of us sat at the end and were virtually unable to talk with the people from the church. It wasn't until the drive home that I realized that we had had no time to visit with any kind of depth with the members of the church. That was the big structural difference between this experience and the one at Holly Grove. In some ways I felt that our joint sermon was better in Ozark, but not having the opportunity to visit with the people meant that we couldn't really get a feel of what they felt about our message, about their church, about their hopes and fears. We left Ozark aware that much had happened, but feeling somewhat out of touch with what really happened. We had few ways to know the response of the

Home Again

people to what we had shared. All we really had was our intuition, which let us know that we had touched some in some special way.

On the way home, despite our fatigue, we talked and talked. Mother and Dad told me of a couple of situations with Roger that were quite revealing. Years ago Dad had been having a conflict with people in the church in Clarksville. Dad was the District Superintendent, and the church had strong leadership in the "Charismatic Movement," a renewal movement based upon the experience of speaking in tongues. Unfortunately, the leader of the church was an angry man who used the orthodoxy of this renewal movement to condemn anyone who disagreed. Since Dad was not a great supporter of the movement, he was seen as a hostile outsider. A confrontation happened at a Charge Conference, which turned into a major difficulty. Dad was inclined to believe the leader of the movement was harming the church and Dad was taking action to undermine his power. At that time Roger came to Dad to vouch for the good character of the man, but he didn't convince Dad to ease off. He had to use his power to disempower the man. About a half year later the man was told by a father in the church to "Stay away from my daughter, or else!" and was accused of being a peeping Tom, somewhat vindicating Dad for his difficult position.

Then, just a few years ago Roger wrote a letter for the *Arkansas United Methodist* newspaper accusing Hendrix College, the church-sponsored college in Arkansas, of not serving the interests of the church. Mother said, "It really made me mad, so I wrote a letter to the editor rebutting his accusations. Later some of Roger's friends thanked me for my letter, but Roger never told me his response."

I said, "No wonder I felt so uncomfortable, like there was something strained in his hosting of us. Perhaps he wasn't sure he really wanted us to preach in his pulpit. Maybe that's also why we didn't have much time to visit with the parishioners. Maybe he was protecting his people from us." I might have been incorrect in the inferences I was making, but now I understood why I had felt that there was definitely more to our visit and relationship than first met the eye.

The more we talked about it the more we all agreed that there did appear to be some reservation on Roger's part. To me that was more evidence of the importance of this journey. Years later as we remember the meaningful and positive experiences of our lives together, some of the shadow side of our lives still creep in. Conflicts just don't get buried. They either get fully resolved or contaminate something somewhere else. Evidently, the conflicts at Clarksville and over Hendrix College and some theological differences were still alive and well.

Dad and I decided to make sure to have dialog time at future churches. We thought that was the major strategic lesson of this trip, the major thing we could do to enhance the experiences at the next places. Little did we know, but Roger was to reach out to Mother and Dad in a surprising way that would open me up to a more important change.

July 29, 1997

Last week I sent an article from this journal on our Holly Grove experience to the *Arkansas United Methodist*. I also sent a copy to Mother and Dad, and last night Dad called me and said, "Ron, you sure know how to make your father cry." I didn't know what he meant until he referred to the journal. This morning as I have reflected on our conversation I find myself putting myself in the shoes of an older man whose days in the limelight are fading. Instead of being a sort of activist like I am at my age, Dad has become a contemplative. I'm kind of sprinting through this phase of life—doing this, doing that—while Dad is being more receptive and gracious. His call was a blessing to me. Although publishing an article is nice, I find myself satisfied enough with Dad's blessing that publication fades in importance. Once again I feel lucky to have parents who have found enough peace in themselves to genuinely offer their blessing to those who do creative work.

It's interesting to me how freeing it feels to know that my parents will bless work that I do that is true to my deeper self. I realize that I have spent a lot of time trying to do work that is approved of on a grander scale at work or in public that might have really been an attempt to receive my parents' approval and blessing. To receive their blessing and approval without having to have it published or some tangible evidence of high quality means that I can seek publication or success without needing it. I am blessed enough. This frees me up to write and work from an inner drive to express myself, not a neurotic drive to prove that I'm ok. And once I've expressed myself, and a few others have received those expressions, I don't really need to be honored on a grand scale. Such success would be nice but unnecessary.

The truth is that my drive to be successful and honored has diminished as my relationship with my parents has deepened and healed. However, there's a voice in me that asks where my motivation will come from if I'm not driven by a desire to prove myself.

When I was a young up-and-coming runner in college, I was an angry runner. Few of my teammates liked to train with me everyday because I would work so furiously to beat them, even in practice. Because of that angry drive I catapulted to the top of the state's running circles. Then I began to calm down and identify some of my anger, releasing it. At first I was worried that I'd lose my motivation, but to my surprise, I found pure delight in the attempt to run a perfect race. I loved the attempt to run fast with good, relaxed form. My fellow competitors became, instead of enemies, helpers in our mutual attempts to run well. I still wanted to win, but mainly because winning is more fun. I didn't *need* to win anymore. What I became was a runner who was an artist, not just a competitor. When I ran a beautiful race, I usually won, but if I didn't win, I still knew that I had done something beautiful. That's what I think I'm feeling freed to do as I accept my parents' blessing.

August 8, 1997

I called Mother and Dad over some trip plans, but Mother interrupted me to say, "Ron, we've got some important news. Your Dad has been diagnosed with cancer of the esophagus and will be receiving extensive testing and surgery next week." She told me that it was very serious, but they had met the surgeon, whom they really liked. She said that cancer of the esophagus is usually fatal because it's the kind of cancer that normally has no symptoms until it has progressed beyond cure. But since Dad had been having some stomach and esophagus problems for a few years, doctors had been checking on him every six months. They caught the cancer, Mother and Dad were told, at its outset and thought it was curable. Mother was the one telling me all this, including Dad's emotional condition. She said he was optimistic and in good spirits, but, she said, "he won't tell anyone, but I can tell that it sometimes really bothers him."

Home Again

Once again I'm struck with who the new caretaker is — Mother, not Dad. Her strength rises up even as Dad's wanes.

Obviously, we won't be going to Pocahontas in a couple of weeks as planned.

I called them often. One day Dad told me that Roger had called him nearly every day, just like he had when Dad was ill just before the Ozark trip. He said, "We may be wrong about Roger, or maybe it's just that our trip there has opened a door that we didn't know was there."

I replied, "Dad, I've been bothered by some of what I've said about Roger. I keep thinking of his expressions of care in contrast to my suspicions about him. You know, I've always had a problem with conservative theology or conservative politics. I'm not the only one in our family who has gotten into arguments with conservatives that have left me feeling furious. I think that when I heard that Roger is more conservative than we are I approached him with some level of scorn and suspicion myself. I think I saw the speck in his eye despite the log in my own.

"For someone whose profession is creating an atmosphere of acceptance in my counseling work, sometimes I sure do have trouble accepting certain people.

"Then someone like Roger comes along who fits all my stereotypes except one: he reaches out to you with such a caring spirit that his character rises above my expectations."

Dad's response was minimal then, but I couldn't help but remember how often he had told me of the same struggle he had with men and women who differed with him and his views. Somehow he had found a way to convey respect, though. One of his best friends, his old seminary roommate, Clarence Snelling, once told me, "Your dad is a man who has somehow been able to be friends with people who were polar opposites to his point of view. He could love the racist, the conservative, the chauvinist in a way that I could never do. He was able to minister to people in places where I would have been run out of town. That is truly a gift."

Maybe Roger had been more open to Dad than to me, for perhaps Roger sensed my judgmentalness and was worried about what *I* might say, not Dad.

So I was struck with an insight that didn't make me smell too good, even if it might be good for me.

I have a friend who often says about such experiences, "Don't you just hate it when that happens?"

Home Again

Chapter Five
UP ON THE ROOF

For the second time in two months Dad's illness had brought up questions about aging and mortality. He was 71 years old. I was 46. The last three years had been a time when, for the first time in my life, I had been feeling myself age. I couldn't run as fast anymore—obviously so. I had just gotten glasses for the first time. I kept having aches and pains that lingered on. I didn't feel close to death, but Dad's illness and my aging had me musing about life, youth, aging, and death.

Maybe that's why, in the late spring I decided to strip and re-roof my house myself. Maybe I just wanted to prove that I was young enough to still do it.

I had done roofing work when I was 27. It's not work that requires much skill, just strength and daring. At 27 I had both. The pitch of the roof didn't frighten me, the heat of the sun didn't faze me much, and the hard, dirty work was just work. I still remembered the simple skills, and I still wasn't afraid of hard work and heat, so I figured I could do it and save a few thousand dollars.

On the roof of our house were three layers of shingling, so I'd have to strip it. I bought a flat-headed shovel, some tar paper and nails, and climbed onto the roof. Beginning on the easy part of the roof where the slope was gentle, I made good progress. I hired three 14 year old boys, including my son, to help me, and they were amazed at how much more efficient I was than they were—and I was wishing I hadn't offered to pay them so much money, they were so slow. But we were getting the work done, and I was beginning to think that I didn't feel 46 after all.

Then I got to the steep pitch.

Ron McDonald

I didn't slip. I just was afraid I would. On this part of the roof, I was slower than boys were on the easy part. Of course, they wouldn't touch the tough part, so I was stuck with a job that I'd have to get used to.

Darn. I couldn't get used to it. I thought a lot of how I used to do the job when I was 27. I used to imagine falling from the roof and how I would land feet first, bounce and roll, wash off the scratches, rub the bruise, maybe have to have a tetanus shot, then go back to work. Now I thought of hitting the ground, breaking a bone or two, rolling around in pain, and spending a few days in the hospital. And not even a hot bath would help.

Dad asked me how I was doing with it, and I confessed that some parts were quite slow. "You're not as young as you used to be, huh?" he'd tease me.

I didn't think it was funny. I told him, "Remember that old bumper sticker on the back of an old, slow truck on a winding mountainous road—'I may be slow, but I'm ahead of you'?"

He'd laugh and say, "Yeah, but I'm smart enough to hire someone who goes faster than you!"

Smart aleck.

I was discouraged. Still, I climbed back up onto the roof. Working slowly, my next door neighbor, Wally, a 27 year old man I sometimes ran with, was suddenly underneath me. "Ron," he said. "How's it going?"

"Kind of tough," I confessed.

"You're making good progress," he offered.

"Yeah, I have been." I left off the "but…" that I felt.

He said, "I just left a job and will be taking another one soon. So I'm between jobs, and I've done a lot of roofing. I'd love to help you and let you pay me what you think I'm worth."

Home Again

Contrary to Dad's opinion of my intelligence, I'm not dumb enough not to know when God just offered me salvation. "Yeah, I could use some help," I calmly replied, hiding my absolute elation (after all, roofers and baseball players aren't supposed to cry). And my neighbor got his tools and started to work with me.

He was good at it. And he was 27. Steep pitches didn't scare the hell out of him!

Besides, I was the boss, so I could delegate. I gave him the steep pitches, and I took the other parts.

Things went a lot faster with Wally helping. I liked him, too. He talked to me like I was his father, telling me his personal story while he saved me from fear and possible hospitalization. Good trade-off, I rationalized, until I couldn't anymore. Then I started paying him better.

I told my dad that God just took care of me because I'm such a good person.

"No," he replied, "you're just lucky!"

One day Wally and I stripped the roof just above Susan's and my bedroom, a room we had just painted and redecorated. By the end of the day we were tired, and since it hadn't rained in weeks, I checked the forecast, and seeing that there was but a mere 20% chance of rain for the night, we figured it would be safe not to cover it under the next morning.

Tired and dirty, I bathed and went to bed early.

About 3 AM I awoke to do something 27 year old men don't have to do. There in the bathroom, eyes half closed, I thought I saw a flicker of light. I thought about it for a few seconds, then suddenly my eyes popped open with fear. Was that lightning? I thought I heard thunder.

I walked quickly to the back door and looked to the southwest where storms usually come from, hoping that

that was just someone down at the river at 3 AM shooting off fireworks.

It wasn't.

There was a storm heading my way.

I put on my running shoes and ran over to Wally's house and started pounding on his door.

No answer.

The wind was picking up. I felt a sprinkle.

I ran home, opened the workshop, got a tarp and a few tools, and climbed up the ladder onto the roof.

But the part I had to cover was Wally's part. It was steep. Very steep!

The sprinkles were turning into rain.

I thought about my 46 year old body climbing on that part of the roof with rain drops making it even more slippery.

Then I thought of my wife, Susan, sleeping in that just redecorated bedroom.

And I thought of that dangerous roof.

And I thought of what Susan might do to me if that newly decorated bedroom was destroyed by my laziness.

It was raining a bit harder. And there was a lot of thunder and lightning.

I shimmied out onto that part of the roof, carrying the tarp with me—something made me feel like 27 again. On the other side of the peak was a roof ladder we had made that Wally wasn't afraid to use. I laid the tarp down, draped it over part of the roof, put the ladder over it to hold it down, just as the rain started coming down *hard*. Quickly, I shimmied back across the peak, unrolling the tarp with me, until it covered the whole exposed roof. All I had left to do was tack it down so that the increasingly violent winds wouldn't blow it off, then I could get off the roof and out of the thunderstorm.

Home Again

I had forgotten my hammer.

The wind was blowing so hard that I knew if I let go and went to get my hammer, it would blow the tarp off the roof immediately, and it was raining so hard now that if the tarp were off for even a minute, the bedroom would be soaked.

I sat there getting soaked by rain, surrounded by wind, flashes of lightning, and the sound of loud thunder above the roof of my house, wearing running shorts and running shoes and tried to think of something else to do.

As I thought of Susan sleeping below me and the lightning above me, I decided to do what any insane man would do in such circumstances. I lay down on the roof, straddling the roof valley, and with my body, held down the tarp to keep the rain off Susan.

And I prayed. I prayed, "God, I know we need the rain, but if you don't mind making it rain hard for just a short time, I'd appreciate it. And if you do see fit that I get hit by lightning, please just give me a small jolt. Maybe just the right amount to juice up my sex life a little."

That didn't help much, so I started reciting the 23rd Psalm. Until I got to the part about "the valley of the shadow of death," which, lying in the roof's valley, didn't make me feel much better. So I stopped.

It was a windy thunderstorm, for sure, but I was keeping the rain out of the bedroom, I could see.

It only lasted 30 minutes. Long ones, for sure, but who was I to complain when it stopped? As quickly as it came, it left.

The winds died down, too, and I finally climbed out of the valley, got my hammer, and tacked down the now unneeded tarp.

I climbed down the ladder, stood on our back porch for a bit, legs shaking, then sighed and had a great revelation:

this'll make a great story, I thought! Only no one will believe me. No, they might believe *me*.

I walked into the house, my hair plastered down like a wet cat, my shoes squeaking on the floor, and went into Susan's and my bedroom. Susan was awake. She switched on the light, looked at me, and, with eyes wide open, asked, "*Ronald*, you weren't on the roof in this thunderstorm, were you?"

When Susan calls me Ronald I know one of two things is going to happen: either I'm in big trouble or something good is about to happen. I wasn't sure what "Ronald" meant this time.

I looked at the floor and nodded yes.

"Oh, Ronald, I've just been *praying* that you weren't up there!"

Now, my friends and family know Susan. If they heard Susan say she was praying for someone they'd know right off that she *really* has a soft spot for that person. That person was me! I sighed and smiled and knew what to say.

"Yeah, I was. I got hit by lightning, too. You wanna know what it did to me?"

I jumped into bed.

Dad called about something the next day. Susan answered the phone and told him what I'd done the night before — on the roof, that is.

Ever since then, whenever I've teased Dad for some mistake, he's said, "Yeah, but at least I'm smart enough to come in out of the rain."

But, hey, I did climb around up there like I was still 27.

Chapter Six

ILLNESS

August 17, 1997

With Dad about to go into the hospital for major surgery for a life-threatening illness, we gathered together as a whole family for the baptism of Amy and Maya, my brother Tom's and his wife Junko's two children. Dad called me last week saying, "Tom thinks I'm going to die from this, so he wants me to baptize his children beforehand." I laughed, but didn't have my usual smart-aleck response. It was too close to my fears. The gathering was just our immediate family, and for the first time in maybe 20 years all six of Mother's and Dad's sons showed up with all but one child from our families (the seventh, David Driver, whom we adopted, died in 1992). We've had five of us six at many gatherings, but to have all six of us and our families was momentous.

We sat around in the afternoon with two curious things happening. One was that Mother, who had also been asked to lead the baptism service, was spending her time preparing for her part in the leadership. That had always been Dad's role in our home. She was the one who was looking up hymns, talking about plans and obviously feeling honored to have been asked. The other was that Dad was holding court with us, giving and receiving affectionate insults. His calm and caring before the coming life-threatening operation was so strong that we didn't spend our time talking about him and our hopes for his survival. The afternoon was about Amy and Maya.

This was a crucial event in the life of our family. We were affirming the life of our father at the point where death was knocking on his door by honoring his and Mother's offspring and the hope they carry with them.

I had brought my guitar, so I led the singing, then Dad baptized the children and Mother led the family in our vows to the children and Tom and Junko. There were two highlights in the ceremony. One was the fact that Mother and Dad had changed the usual United Methodist ceremony so that it was accepting of other faiths out of respect for Junko's Buddhist heritage. In fact, Junko had recently taken Amy and Maya to her childhood home in Japan with her earlier in the summer to visit her parents, and, while there, the children were blessed in the Buddhist tradition. So this service of ours was like a second "baptism." They used words like "God the Creator, God the Sustainer, and God the Holy Spirit." I felt proud to be part of a family that is able to affirm the universality of the Spirit, not having to hold up our tradition as the only way.

The second highlight was Mother's doing. In all the years I've known Mother I don't ever recall having seen her appear choked up in public. I could always tell when she was emotional, for she would act a bit nervous and smile a lot, but she is pretty stoic. This time, as she shared some thoughts about baptism and parenting, without her old nervous smile, she became choked up, struggling to go on. It reached deep inside of me. This was part of the magic, too. She was taking the mantle of leadership from her husband at this time of crisis, showing her emotional depth, her great love for him and the family. Her years of being the behind-the-scenes person had weathered her into a wise old woman. She was not only full of wisdom and confidence, but now unashamed to disclose her strong feelings. It reminds me of that one phrase in the Bible when Jesus heard of an untimely death—"and Jesus wept."

My mother wept.

Afterwards we went to David's house and ate. Dad was having to fast prior to surgery, so he had to put up with a lot of people telling him how delicious the food was. He referred to it as his "Last Supper." We told him we hoped it was.

Truth is, as I left I wept, too. I couldn't imagine being more ready for his death, but I didn't want it to happen yet anyway.

August 19, 1997

Dad entered surgery today. I called him and he said he had thirty minutes before they would take him out of his room. They'd tested him and drugged him up since yesterday. I asked, "Are you nervous?"

"No, not really," he replied. "I think I've got a great doctor, and I'm ready." (Mother told me he's just hungry, implying that he thinks he'll get to eat sooner if he gets this out of the way.) He was in the room with Jim and Mother and all were joking and laughing. He told me they had rented a hotel room at the hospital where I could sleep when I visited on Wednesday night with Don, but that he expected me to pay my portion of the rent.

I replied, "I would tell you to go to hell but not right now, I guess." We laughed, and I said, "I love you, Dad. Goodbye."

He said, "I love you, too, Ron."

I hung up, and smiling, told my colleague, Kim Campbell, who had just arrived for work, of the circumstances. Still half laughing at the jocular conversation, I was aware that I was also tearful. Kim asked me if I was open to a prayer. I was, and I'm glad I was. Praying for him and me, and for Kim's recovering sister, meant a lot.

August 20, 1997

Last night we got word of good reports from the surgeon, despite a huge amount of internal restructuring that would require a great deal of recovery and probably cause Dad a lot of pain in a couple of days when they would lower the painkiller dosage. The doctor said he thought they had caught the cancer at its outset and tests indicated they had gotten it all. This afternoon Don and I would drive to Little Rock and pay him and Mother a visit.

August 29, 1997

For the last week Mother, my brothers, my son, Jonah, and I have been staying with Dad in the hospital as he recovered from the surgery. The details of the massive work they did on his internal organs and the amount of cutting and scarring was incredible. According to pathology reports they took out the cancer completely and he could expect to recover, with some limitations. He spent nearly a week in intensive care, and, while sleeping, after twice pulling out the stomach drainage tube that entered his nose, they asked us to stay with him and "slap his hand" if he tried to do it again. His sleep was fitful, pain-filled, and sometimes even led to "Acute Care Psychosis." My brother, Don, who is a psychiatrist, explained to us that such a condition is common for patients in Intensive Care Units.

One night he became quite agitated with the idea that Linda Driver, his adopted daughter-in-law, was one of the nurses and was mistreating him. It took some time for Jim and Mother to convince him that he had been hallucinating. After a few of those disoriented times, they moved him to a room with natural light to help him know daylight from night.

Ever since Susan and I had our children, I have been amazed at the healing power of sunlight. With both our boys, we held them naked in sunlight as a way of treating possible jaundice. Since then I've learned much about sunlight and moods, and found myself feeling so much more energy and happiness "when the sun shines bright." Science has been proving sunlight's healing qualities, but common sense has known it as long as humans have existed. In Quakerism we talk about "being held in the Light." In a sense that's what the doctor ordered for Dad. And the room and its light did help him find his bearings.

August 31, 1997

Yesterday was Mother's birthday. She has spent most of 12 days now nursing Dad in the hospital through this surgery, which has been more successful and complications-free than anyone expected. Dad has been in constant pain, sometimes at a high level, sometimes just uncomfortable. I've been taking shifts with my brothers sitting with him at night. He sleeps in short naps, awakens, then needs to be moved, take some ice into his mouth, or other simple needs. He's been an ideal patient. He's direct about his needs, pleasant with everyone, and doesn't complain about extraneous matters. Mother has stayed with him during the days, but we've made sure to spell her at night. It's tiring enough in the day.

The other day a client of mine said, "My family's motto seems to be 'There's always something.'" He said it with bitterness and despair. I replied, "That's true. There always is some other problem. The way you handle that fact determines whether it's a problem to be cursed or one to be solved." Then I thought of my own family in relation to this crisis. Because of our commitment to one another and openness with one another, we've laid the foundation for such a crisis to bring us closer together rather than drive us apart.

When I was in college and seminary I became fascinated with the meaning of faith. I found that I could not understand what the apostle Paul meant about faith when I equated faith with belief. I began to understand that faith has more to do with radical openness, which is virtually the opposite of belief. Faith opens us up to the world, to life, to one another. Beliefs may be a rich source of security, but beliefs, by definition, close off other ideas and experiences. We join others who believe like we do to feel a part of something exclusive. None of us is strong enough to do without beliefs, but that doesn't mean that beliefs have the same kind of meaning as does faith. Faith is so radical that we can't live by faith constantly. We use beliefs to prop up our waning faith. Faith opens us up. Faith provides a different kind of security—security that is independent of our need for predictability and commonness. Beliefs provide a more worldly kind of security, not the other-worldly security faith offers.

The trouble with belief systems, however, is that just around the corner from them is an opposing system that makes good sense. Faith can adjust to such challenge. Beliefs cannot.

Dad's illness is such a challenge on a small scale. Here I am believing that our journey back to our home churches is ordained by God, then Dad gets sick with a life-threatening illness that may halt this journey before it is completed. I find myself wondering if this really is that important. Maybe I've fooled myself again into believing that something is actually important when it really isn't that big of a deal. Well, it has been a big deal to me, but I was beginning to believe it might be a big deal to plenty of others as well. Maybe Roger's resistance to our visit was a more accurate portrayal of the truth: that this is but one more Sunday among many, not a major event for his parish. Such doubts are part of this for me. They re-ground me, helping me keep this in perspective.

I remember reading years ago that Harry Stack Sullivan, a great psychoanalytic theoretician and therapist, said that a therapist could only expect one thing from the work of therapy—a paycheck. A few years later I found in Sheldon Kopp's writings the one other thing I've found as reward for my work—fun. I can have fun and receive a paycheck. I think of those ideas now when my doubts bother me. Despite the possible insignificance of these trips to others, they are definitely fun for me. In some ways, that's enough.

And the truth is that despite Dad's illness, because of the way my family was surrounding him and working together, this was kind of fun. At least it was very meaningful. I think that our family was functioning on faith at this time. We were open with one another, open to the emerging strengths and weaknesses, open to the emotions, letting the process run its course. So out of this crisis was coming a golden opportunity that our faith, our openness, would allow us to fully experience. Out of this curse came a blessing.

"There's always something," can be said with negativity and disillusionment, or with a smile and wonderment. What might the next 'something' be? I'll definitely learn something from it.

Part of what was special about this time was that seeing Dad recover so well from this was a testament to the importance of the Spirit in healing. I've rarely seen a person or our family so well tuned in to the importance of the Spirit in this process. More than ever we were watching for the movement of the Spirit. What is that phenomenon? It is the essence of the heart. We were listening with our hearts. The week before when Dad went through the Acute Care Psychosis, seeing people who weren't there, getting angry at mistreatment that wasn't happening, the family response was informed by our knowledge of delusions and such, but determined by the heartfelt calm that let us know that this was part of the process of recovery. The Spirit was giving us the strength to help Dad relax and understand the truth. And in a few hours, Jim and Mother were able to help him understand that his mind was playing tricks on him. Because of their calm comfort and his deep trust in the family, he was able to relax and move back into the place where his inner peace could contribute to his healing. Only the Spirit has that impact. Only when one can be trusting enough to listen openly — faithfully — can the Spirit's peace provide such calm.

As I write this, fully aware of the probable next trip to Little Rock, the loss of most of another night's sleep, the fatigue the next day, and the difficulty of concentrating the next day with all these thoughts about Dad, Mother, and my brothers, I feel so fortunate to have this happening. Once again, we are being given an experience that will become a part of our wisdom. Mother and Dad are showing us how to grow old gracefully, how to face death, how to accept help. And we are showing them and our children how to care for one another throughout life. I sure am lucky!

Home Again

He spent a month in the hospital. Mother was with him everyday, and one of the rest of us, sons and grandchildren, was with him every night. It would take six months to recover. He would lose 40 or 50 pounds (to the weight he always wanted to be!), look 10 years older, but never waver from his desire to live and see the next thing happen in our family. "I've got to live to see Jonah and Rebecca and Scott graduate," he'd say, then add, "Then I'll want to see Maya and Malachi go to kindergarten, and Betsy march in the Razorback band and then Jesse play high school baseball. In fact, I guess there'll always be something worth living for!"

I once asked him his feelings about dying. Immediately, he replied, "Oh, I'm sure it'll be OK. What I don't want is to be a burden on anyone."

When he got home after those painful and difficult weeks in the hospital, he told us all, one at a time, that he had broken down and wept at the incredible love and care that had surrounded him. He said, "When I first came home from that month in the hospital, I sat down with Lois and started crying. I kept thinking about how much care I had received. I was never alone. Y'all gave up nights and did all that traveling, and Lois set aside her own physical problems to be with me. I kept asking, 'Why would they do all that?' It really meant a lot to me. It didn't really hit me until I sat down at home and thought about it."

I replied, "Dad, I was glad at how well we all coordinated our efforts, too. And we've been talking about your time in the hospital. We've been amazed that despite all the pain and discomfort you had, *not one of us* heard you complain one time about something that we couldn't do anything about. That's inspiring to us." He cried in response.

Chapter Seven

ON THE ROAD AGAIN – TO POCAHONTAS

In 1959 we moved to Pocahontas, a "big" town of 3800 people in northeast Arkansas. In the foothills of the Ozark Mountains, and a way-station on Highway 67 from Little Rock to St. Louis, Pocahontas, like all small towns in the south in the 50s, was surrounded by farms. But industry was big in Pocahontas. Shoes and baseball bats were made in factories there. For kids baseball was king in Pocahontas. During the three years we lived there, the high school football team did not win one game. Maybe because of the baseball bat factory, baseball was the community recreation, and the teams were good. Pocahontas was a north Arkansas town—people weren't as immediately friendly like southern Arkansas townsfolks. It was a town more rooted in individualism and timeclocks. The Methodist Church was on a hill near the town square, but did not play quite as prominent a role in the town's life as the churches in Holly Grove and Ozark.

March 16, 1998

Two weeks ago Dad told me he was ready to schedule our third trip—to Pocahontas. I called the minister there, Steve Wingo, and we scheduled a trip for March 29.

A week later Dad called to talk with me about his plans for his part of our sermon. It was an important conversation to me. It gave me more insight into the impact of this journey on Dad. His imagination and memories have been deeply sparked by this journey back. He said he wants to reach into the meaning of Jacob's dream at Bethel in Genesis (28:10-22). This is the dream of "Jacob's Ladder" in which Jacob sees the impact of his descendents on humankind and erects a monument to his vision called Bethel, which means house of God. I can't help but see the significance of this story to Dad.

Here he is now: old, nearing death, dependent on others to encourage him and sometimes nurse him, and choosing a biblical text filled with hope for what he has passed on to humankind. He told me he wanted to express to the congregation in Pocahontas his belief that that church was a house of God, one that touched our lives. As Jacob exclaimed, "Surely the Lord is in this place, and I was not aware of it." He talked about wanting to tie his thoughts into his theme of the cross. I don't think he was fully aware of the connection this text had to his life now. It was like his spiritual self was choosing this for him.

I have often reflected on how great souls often receive a new name. Gandhi was named "The Mahatma." King called himself "a drum major for justice." Jacob was renamed "Israel." Fathers receive a new name as well— Dad or Daddy. Part of our destiny and our blessing is tied up in the renaming we receive. My dad has fathered a generation of good people. None are perfect, just as Israel's offspring was not perfect. But Dad took his fathering seriously enough to pass on a generation of seekers and doers.

The next time we talked he told me some of what he wanted to say about Abraham and the dream at Bethel. I knew he meant Jacob, but I ribbed him about it, saying, "You never did read the Bible." He laughed briefly, said,

"Smart aleck," and went on. In that moment I knew that despite his humor I had embarrassed him. He did not like the fact that he makes more mistakes with names and details now. I had ribbed him about something that wasn't all that funny to him.

When we finished our conversation I told my wife, Susan, "This is so important to Dad. I have all sorts of distractions like work and children, but this journey is the focus of his life now." I felt almost as if I was fathering my father. Just as my children looked to me so intensely to develop their sense of the world, I sensed this journey was partly about Dad leaning on me to provide a means for his passing on some items of great spiritual importance.

More than ever I saw the sense in calling this last stage of life "passing on." Dad was obviously passing on physically, less obviously he was spiritually moving into new rooms — new Bethels.

A few years ago I was the interim pastor at a United Methodist Church named Bethel. It was an African American church and I, being a white man, was welcomed by most and not welcomed by a few. Instead of black preaching, they had to listen to my stories, which I believe they sincerely liked, but it was not the excited, spirit-filled, cadence-filled preaching they were used to. That experience had a profound impact on both me and the church. The church, having had a good but not perfect experience with a white pastor, was able to merge with a mostly white congregation to develop a fully integrated church — integrated in fact and form. By form I mean that they drew from white and black worship traditions and merged them effectively. It is a church that's still alive and thriving. Their first pastor was white. Their second was black. Their congregation is white and black.

Home Again

It changed me because I knew that I had developed the ability to be bi-cultural, something I had wanted ever since the integration days of the 60s. This is the ability to appreciate and participate comfortably in two cultures. Black people are naturally bi-cultural, for they have to be to make it in the dominant white culture. White people can stay mono-cultural if they want, however. That mono-cultural slant is part of what keeps our society racist. Mother and Dad planted a seed in me years ago to want to turn my back on racism, and becoming bi-cultural was, I knew, a big step in that direction. My experience at Bethel helped me break some of the biggest chains of racism I have carried.

One Sunday at Bethel Mother and Dad were visiting. I preached a sermon on sacrifice that got the congregation pretty excited. I spoke enthusiastically of a woman who dove to the aid of her toddler son who was in the process of knocking a pot of boiling water off the stove. Shoving her son away, she took the full spill on her leg. The doctor told her she would have a bad scar, but she told me, "Funny thing was, despite the way it looked, it never hurt, and it healed perfectly." In the context of my sermon, talking about the spiritual call to self-sacrifice, the congregation erupted when I closed the story. I could see as well that Mother and Dad were deeply affected by what was happening—both because of the sermon they were hearing and because of how the congregation was responding.

Bethel, of course, is a central part of the story Dad is focusing on for Pocahontas. He did not remember the name of that church until I told him, but for me it was another example of the unconscious and spiritual interplay happening between us. I believe that Dad chose that biblical text in part because of our common experience at my Bethel.

March 29, 1998

I drove to Pocahontas feeling well prepared for my part of the sermon. There had been a tragedy in Jonesboro, Arkansas, a 45 minute drive from Pocahontas, that focused my thinking. Four children and a teacher were killed by two young boys shooting at them after setting off a false fire alarm. The teacher, Shannon Wright, used her body to shield a child from bullets and died. (Flags along the way were flying at half mast.) That supreme sacrifice is one that none of us wants to be faced with, for if we flinch the moment will pass and the person we would protect will be harmed. None of us know if we have that kind of instantaneous courage. That sacrificial love is what I planned to preach about. I told Dad that I wanted to talk about how he has given of himself over these years in a way that has been the kind of gradual sacrifice of self that is the one way we can choose each day.

A funny thing happened when sharing this compliment with Dad. The Arkansas bishop recently referred to Dad as one of the elder "saints" in the United Methodist Church, so Dad has been tooting his horn with that compliment. Every chance he gets he says, with a mischievous smile, "The bishop says I'm a saint."

I said, "I was thinking of the idea of a noble sacrifice—not 'my dad, the saint.'"

He laughed and replied, "I thought you were going to compliment me."

I said, "I couldn't quite do it."

Home Again

He laughed heartily and said, "I can't either!"

"Well," I chimed in, "I'm not going to unless you do!"

"I guess you learned it from me," he added.

As I walked home yesterday afternoon I thought to myself how much like Dad I am. I have no problem sharing deeply felt gratitude toward Dad from the pulpit, but on a private phone call I have to mess with him as I do it. Dad used to share his deepest feeling about his love for us in public prayers and sermons, as if was easier to be complimentary in that context than face to face. Darn. I'm just like my dad!

Pocahontas is a town with three distinct sections. We were staying southeast of the Black River, a tributary of the White River that flows into the Mississippi. This section is made up of some houses, a military airport, and a fast-food strip along Highway 67, the main drag through town. We drove across the bridge into the old section of town, with the courthouse square between two intersecting highways. As soon as we drove into the square I could see that old hula hoop contest the Junior and Senior High students were having in 1960 there. I smiled as I thought of the many, many fads I've lived through since then. I think that was the first fad I saw in full swing.

We drove through town, seeking to remember this and that. So much in the center of town was still the same nearly 40 years later. Despite some newer buildings, larger parking lots, and more modern landscaping, it felt as laid back and peaceful as ever. Our home, however, had been moved and replaced with the church's new educational building and a parking lot. We found the old school had been demolished, except for the old gym, and turned into a city park. I attended the second, third, and fourth grades there.

Ron McDonald

I remember those years in school well. Despite the fact that my parents often refer to my third grade teacher as a poor teacher, that's the year I remember best. I think I began to discover some of my own unique gifts that year. Particularly I learned that I was gifted athletically. We became excellent tetherball players, and I sensed that I was one of the best. To this day my older brother, David, and I can play a mean game of tetherball—a game that is virtually unknown to most people we encounter.

We drove on into the newly developed sections of town and saw the upscale places. There was nothing particularly special about those places to me. They looked much like most modern developments with surrounding schools, a country club, garden shops, and a few restaurants nearby.

Back at the motel, we settled down for a couple of hours, then a church member, Ann Holt, arrived at six to take us all to dinner at her daughter's restaurant with her son, a dentist and member of the choir. Ann had retired as editor of the town's newspaper, still working one-half day a week writing a weekly column. She was a sharp-witted, strong woman, a virtual history-book on the people of the town. Mother and Dad and Ann talked a lot about this person and that person, catching up on the missing years. Obviously Ann and her son John enjoyed the reminiscing as much as Mother and Dad enjoyed the stories she had to tell. At their age, of course, much of the information was about who was living, when they retired, who had died, and what ailed whom.

I have been told that people become more spiritual after they reach their 40s, but from what I see people talk more about their physical health as they get older. Actually, the way it goes is this: young adults talk about physical looks, middle-aged people talk about mental health, and older people talk about illness and death. That's when we're staying on neutral ground (to avoid arguments). Since we were being polite, illness and death were the topics.

Sunday began with us arriving at the church before eight o'clock. Steve Wingo, the pastor had not yet arrived, so we wandered through the church. I set up my dulcimer and guitar and checked the tuning. I met an interesting man, whose name I've forgotten, who takes care of the video for a closed circuit television broadcast of the eleven o'clock service. Friendly and very cooperative, he seemed to be particularly proud of his role with the church. He would look at me like he wanted to say something but didn't quite have the words, and when I spoke he listened like he was hanging on my every word. There was something about his demeanor that led me to think he was a simple man who had found a means of service that was a high calling. His respectful attitude towards me was contagious. I found myself thinking that he was an unknown saint. He said, "I worship at the eight-thirty service, then work at the eleven o'clock one. I like to hear the sermon the second time, though. It makes more sense the second time, and it's always a little different."

I can't, of course, know the circumstances of his weekly life, but unlike most people he seemed to be one of those rare persons who had found a deeply gratifying role in life, something that was of great service to his community.

I once had a job as the director of a counseling center. As the Director I had to hob-nob with wealthy donors, lead marketing efforts, manage staff, etc. At first I was enamored with it—the prestige and power, in particular. Then I began to get in over my head. Although not exactly a country bumpkin, I am also not a society person, and I kept feeling out of place with Memphis society people.

Ron McDonald

Although I'm sometimes a good speaker, I'm more of an entertainer than a salesperson, so I wasn't very good at marketing. Also, I'm not organized enough to manage much more than myself particularly well. When I finally saw myself out of place and returned full time to pastoral counseling, I began to think that I had stepped out of my station in life while in that role. That's a politically incorrect phrase ("station in life") unless seen as a mirror of the gifts we have been given. My gifts were simply not in line with that position. I'm called to be a healer, an enchanter, and a minister to youth. I forgot that for a while.

That man at the church seemed to have a grasp of his calling and be satisfied with it. Would that we all had such integrity.

He also reminded me of a handicapped man named John McCroskey, who kept in touch with me periodically, as if I was his anchor. He wrote me a note once, saying, "Dr. McDonald, I want to be a hero. Can you help me be a hero?"

I couldn't answer that question for about two years, then I come upon an insight. There are two types of heroes: Shannon Wright, the teacher in Jonesboro is one type. She displayed the sudden, spontaneous act of courage that was clearly heroic. The other type is the person who does a small, good deed every day for years and years. One day this person is "discovered" by a reporter, who does a story, and the person is honored for heroism. This is the long-term hero that we should all strive to be.

So two years after John asked my help, I pulled him aside one day and told him that I had figured out how he could be a hero—do something good every day and someday you'll be a hero. Ever since then he's delivered

Home Again

the local paper the *Memphis Flyer* to me and another Church Health Center employee every Wednesday.

And now I've written about him. I guess that means he's a genuine hero!

The audio-visual man in Pocahontas is such a hero, I think.

Worship was particularly meaningful at both services. I felt that our sermons blended together well, and Dad spoke with deep conviction. I could tell that his ordeal with illness, surgery, and recovery had added a new dimension of emotion to his message. His words about Bethel were not nearly so meaningful as the implicit conviction behind those words. We could sense that he truly felt that his life had been lived in a holy place.

I felt moved to express two things. Talking about sacrifice and courage I told the congregation of my brothers' and my astounding revelation about Dad: during his stay in the hospital he had never complained about anything we couldn't do something about. As I looked at Dad when I said that, I saw him choke up and his lips quiver. I love him.

The second thing that happened came in response to the good choir who sang for us in the second service. Listening to them sing, Dad and I both commented that it reminded us that the church choir in Pocahontas was one of the best we had ever heard—certainly for the small church. So when we got around to time for me to lead "We are Climbing Jacob's Ladder," a song not easy to do accompanied with a guitar, one that we botched royally at the early service, I said, "Now that I remember how well this church sings, I think I need to lead you in the song I lead best: "Down By the Riverside." Which we sang with great depth and feeling.

I've found that each time I am a leader in a strange church worship, I inevitably botch up one part of the service, like we did with "Jacob's Ladder" in the first service. It used to bother me, but now it simply reminds me that I'm a visitor and their ways are theirs. It's become more of a sense of amusement to me now than embarrassment.

One of my funniest *faux pas* was when I was co-leading Episcopal worship. I was helping with communion, and after we finished, the priest, Jim Coleman (now a bishop), gave me one of the two cups of wine, and said, "Will you take care of this one?" Then he quaffed the small amount left in his cup. I looked into mine, and was startled to see the large goblet over half full. I thought, I guess I have to drink it all. I did, but upon chugging it down, I looked at Jim and he whispered, "You didn't have to drink it *all*."

I still had a sermon to preach, too.

The Pocahontas church, like Holly Grove, had a pot luck meal for us. Dad introduced me and said I had a story to tell. "But don't believe a word he says!" he warned them.

I asked them,

Has anyone here ever heard of Dead Horse Gulch?

I used to go fishing with friends at a creek somewhere west of here near Dead Horse Gulch. Every time we went to the creek just to explore without our fishing poles we'd see huge fish in the water. Every time we took our poles with us the fish would disappear. I used to think those fish would hide at the sight of fishing poles. Probably the smartest fish in the world.

To get to the creek we had to walk through a large field and crawl under a barbed wire fence. Just on the field side of the fence was a huge, round pit. At the bottom of the pit were some very large bones.

As we stood gaping at those bones, the older boys would tell us how they got there. They said that there used to be a giant horse that galloped through the countryside killing and eating cows. It must have been the only cow-eating horse that ever existed.

Farmers were appropriately alarmed with the horse, so they got together and dug this big pit that we were looking at. They figured the horse might fall into the pit, break its leg and die. One day a farmer came up on the horse just after it had killed another cow and was about to eat it. The startled horse ran off and as it glanced back at the enraged farmer, it fell into the pit, broke its leg, and died.

And I knew this was true because I was standing there looking at dem bones!

Dad came forward next and told these stories.

This spot where I'm standing used to be the location of the parsonage where we lived back in 1958 through 1961. Just down the street, just to our right, the street was gravel back then. One afternoon I bet Ron—who never wore shoes, whom we called 'RPM' because those are his initials and he never stopped moving—I bet Ron a quarter that he couldn't run up that gravel road and back barefoot. He did it with no problem! He was always a hardheaded and tough-footed boy.

Now he's a liar as well!

One day Lois was in the house with a sprained ankle, unable to move but at a snail's pace. David, Don, and Ron were outside playing. David got in the car and made a scene of making sure the parking brake was on. When he got out, Don, having seen his older brother fiddle with the parking brake, decided he could too. But he let the brake off. The car rolled out of the driveway and curved across the street into our neighbor's, the Bennett's, front steps.

When Lois heard the crash, she sprung up out of bed and, sprained ankle and all, sprinted across the street. Upon seeing that no one was hurt, she drove the car back into our driveway. It didn't hurt the steps, but it sure did damage our car!

We loved Pocahontas, but we lived here at a time when there were statewide difficulties. Governor Faubus was threatening to close all the state's schools to avoid integration. I was really disturbed by that, and I used to wonder what we should do. Our children did go to school here, but I thought seriously about leaving the state.

There was a black teacher at the black school whom I had befriended named Edna McDonald. She was an exceptional woman that I deeply respected. One Saturday she called me and asked if we could talk. I went to her home and she told me that she had just returned from taking her class of elementary kids to the Memphis Zoo on Thursday, the so-called "colored day" when blacks were allowed into the zoo. After visiting the zoo she took her children into Overton Park to eat their sack lunches. Two big, white policemen came up to the children, spoke harshly at them, and demanded that they get back on their bus and leave the park.

Ms. McDonald told me that the ride back to Pocahontas was very quiet. Then she said, "Brother McDonald, I don't know how I can teach my kids to be respectful of the law and white people when they are treated like that. Would you come talk with my kids sometime?"

I agreed to, and was the speaker at their elementary school graduation that spring. I spoke about Shadrack, Meshak, and Abendigo, saying that these were men of great faith, examples to us of how our faith can take us safely through hard times, even times when we are being mistreated, making us into better people.

I've always hoped that my presence at that school gave those mistreated children a better experience, one that would perhaps offer healing after the wounding in Memphis.

I'll never forget that experience here.

After worship a church member, John Jackson, the President of the Bank of Pocahontas, invited us to the local country club for lunch. He took us north of town to a idyllic place where we sat down with about six others, and after talking politely and lightly, began to share some more important stories from the past.

Dad again referred to the issues of race that were looming over the state at the time, and John told this story.

> We never thought much about race, even though years later I could see it was wrong to force black children to ride over an hour to Newport to high school each day. We thought we had decent race relations here, maybe because there weren't too many blacks in town. We once asked the local black leaders in the early 60s if they wanted to integrate into our school, and they turned us down. We thought at the time it was because they liked segregation, but now I figure it was because they were scared to. I don't blame them, either.

But our baseball team was integrated. Once we traveled into Missouri to a tournament. On the way home we stopped at a restaurant and the manager said he wouldn't serve those boys—pointing to our black teammates. We just all got up and left, and came back to Pocahontas where we could all eat together.

I didn't think much of that then, but I'm kind of proud of it now.

I hugged Mother and Dad after lunch, then we parted ways. They would drive back to Conway, I to Memphis. I had been surprised with the many stories of race relations that had been told. The thought began to materialize in my mind that our experience, particularly Dad's experience, was preparatory for a major defining moment in Dad's life that was ahead in DeWitt. He was being prepared for the racial conflict which would transform many lives through his courage in the town and ministry ahead.

Chapter Eight

DEWITT

But DeWitt's pastor, Levon Post, did not want us to come.

May 12, 1998

I wrote to Levon Post after speaking with him on the phone. He told me he's reluctant to say yes to our proposal without knowing us, so I suggested he talk with Jack Essex or the Hamptons. After the call I decided to write this letter.

Dear Rev. Post:

> I'm writing to follow-up on our conversation last week with some thoughts.
>
> Dad was pastor in DeWitt from 1962-66, a period when the church experienced a serious conflict over how to respond to racial issues. We had a wonderful experience there, making friends that have lasted a lifetime. I was a 5th-8th grader there and remember DeWitt as both a great town to grow up in and a place where we all struggled to come to terms with the liberation movement of African Americans.
>
> Our purpose for going back to our old home churches (Holly Grove, Ozark, Pocahontas, DeWitt, and Rogers) is two-fold. First, we want to represent the passing of the torch of ministry from one generation to the next.

That has been particularly uplifting to us and spawned much response from parents and their children. Second, we want to remember and reminisce with those whom we shared our lives and talk about how it has affected who we are. We feel that our mutual journeys need to lead us all to an affirmation of life as God has given it to us. Our shared faith keeps overcoming our mistakes, even making them into good memories.

Our experience in the first three churches has been very inspiring to us, and the response has been overwhelming. It has really surprised us--obviously we are touching a nerve. Perhaps this transitional culture we live in needs to remember its roots, and we are representing that. That's what we hope for if we come to DeWitt.

I am one of two pastoral counselors here in Memphis with the Church Health Center, a health care clinic for the "working poor" started and directed by a United Methodist minister and family physician. I have been a pastoral counselor for 19 years, and was a college chaplain for six. I attended Hendrix College, Union Theological Seminary in New York, St. Paul School of Theology in Kansas City, and am a Diplomate in the American Association of Pastoral Counselors. Dad has been in the United Methodist ministry since 1949, serving eight charges and twice as District Superintendent. Our time in DeWitt was his only time in the Little Rock Conference. The Bishop refers to him as one of "our saints" a fact that Dad brags about a lot! (I know him better than she does!)

Home Again

I fully understand your reluctance to saying yes to our proposed visit. Dad is well known in the North Arkansas Conference, so those pastors know him well and have quickly consented to our proposal. We respect your authority and will respect your decision.

Should we come to DeWitt, we will address the racial issue that was so important while we were there. At that time the Official Board wrestled with whether or not to allow blacks to be seated were they to visit our church. Carol Hampton and Johnny Schallhorn have both reported to Dad that the discussions around that issue were instrumental in defining how they have worked around racial issues in their careers. It was certainly a central eye-opener for me, and I believe it was a defining moment in Dad's career. We will be especially caring in how we talk about it, however, for, although we believe that remembering is part of faithfulness, remembering without blaming or bitterness is part of gracefulness. I will add that you'll find it to be an incredible story, if you haven't heard it already.

So I hope you find a way for us to visit and share our stories or lead worship some Sunday. We look forward to hearing from you.

In Christ,

Ron McDonald, D.Min.
Pastoral Counselor

cc. Charles McDonald

Ron McDonald

May 21, 1998

After writing Levon two letters, making about 5 phone calls, and talking with him only that once, I received a letter from him today thanking us for the offer to come to DeWitt First Church, but saying, "After thinking carefully about the focus of our church ministry today, I would like to graciously decline your offer."

Dad and I had felt that that would be his decision, and despite some disappointment, we were glad to accept a firm and respectful no. I had tried in vain to get a clear response from him for about a month, so it was nice to get a clear decision. Now we can move on towards Rogers.

Neither of us knows Levon, but our hunch was that he either has some theological difference with us or was wary about dealing with the racial conflicts that were a part of our time there. Either reason was, I thought, a good reason to decline our offer to come. He is the leader of the church, not us.

Nonetheless, upon telling Dad the news, I asked him to go ahead and write for me some of his thoughts and feelings about DeWitt, some of what he might have said there. I decided to dialog on paper with him over these reminiscences.

> Dad: DeWitt was and is a family town. When we moved there our boys were immediately included in the Little League program. The games were in the afternoons because of the mosquitoes. We didn't understand that until the 4th of July. We were taking our boys to swim and were in our bathing suits playing catch at noon because the pool didn't open until 1 p.m. The sun was shining bright and hot and the mosquitoes ate us up!

Home Again

Ron: After we moved to Rogers, where there were no mosquitoes, one of the first things I noticed was that people didn't stand around slapping themselves like they did in DeWitt.

Dad: Worship was a high point for us. Sunday morning the sanctuary was filled and on Sunday night there were almost 100 people. The singing was great. We sang gospel hymns with selections from the congregation. Ron always chose one hymn; I think it was "The Awakening Chorus." Even Lois came and enjoyed Sunday night. (In Pocahontas she stayed home with the little one—that was her excuse.)

Ron: The singing was great, but the music was actually pretty poor! There was, however, one lady with a beautiful voice who would sing "I Come to the Garden Alone." I still love to hear that song, but no one sings it so well.

Dad: There were two small rural churches attached to DeWitt: Prairie Union and Deluce. I went there at 8:30 on Sunday mornings, and then came back to DeWitt. We were able to merge the two churches, moving the Deluce building to Prairie Union—not without problems, but it worked, and we enjoyed the people. They had "pot lucks" with wild game—bear, deer, duck, elk, etc. Our family really enjoyed going there once a month.

Ron: The main things I remember about Prairie Union-Deluce are the vast number of frogs that were there, and you racing a crop duster once as it few next to our speeding station wagon, clocking it at 80 MPH.

Dad: There was a vacant lot next door to the parsonage and we got permission to clear it so the boys and their friends could play baseball and football. The lot was always filled. I took out insurance for passing cars and boys that might get hurt.

Ron McDonald

Ron: When we moved to Memphis, we found a house with a vacant lot beside it that has been the neighborhood playground.

Dad: The parsonage was next door to the church, and Ron and Don practiced their piano lessons in the Educational Building of the church. Lois could hear them and keep an eye on them.

Ron: I'm so glad I had that little bit of piano training. I never found much love in the piano, but I did discover the joy of creating music, which I've never stopped enjoying.

Dad: Our church was particularly focused on family life. We had an excellent Sunday School program, led by Grace Barnett, a great helper and friend to me and to all our family. Then in 1962 Barnes and Ruby Hampton, Jack and Meredith Essex, and Lois and I left 12 children with grandparents to attend the National Family Life Conference in Chicago. It was an inspiration to us all, and we came back to share with our church. The following year we had a Family Life Revival led by Leon Smith of the Family Life Committee of the Methodist Church, whom we had heard in Chicago.

Ron: I still remember Brother Smith's first series of sermons. He was a storyteller. He actually kept my attention — not a small feat for a kid nicknamed RPM. Then the next time I heard him — that might have been in Rogers — he didn't share stories, but thoughts and ideas, and he lost me. I think that's why I tell stories almost all the time rather than teach ideas.

Dad: In 1963 I went to a United Nations workshop in New York City sponsored by the Methodist Church. As we were returning we stopped at Monticello where we asked a man why he was lowering the flag to half-mast. He told us that President Kennedy had been

Home Again

killed. We traveled all night on the bus, stopping to get papers and listen to the reports. It was an emotional time for every one. I still have a copy of my sermon the Sunday following his death. I titled it "It is Hate that Kills." The title was taken from an article in *The Atlanta Constitution*. It was an emotional day for us all, and the church was filled with people—a day I'll never forget.

Ron: I heard about Kennedy's assassination in my seventh grade English class. Some students were exclaiming, "They got that nigger-lover." It upset me a lot.

Dad: We had several missionaries visit us in DeWitt. One we especially enjoyed was W. D. Masters from India. He stayed in our home and made us Indian bread for breakfast. Our church reached out with our own missionaries. Mid and Hamp Hampton went to the Red Bird Mission in Kentucky. They came back and shared with us the work there. Our church sent funds to help the project. Hamp was a pharmacist for them, and Mid taught children there.

Ron: Having people stay in our homes who were from different cultures was incredibly fascinating. It opened me up. Thanks for doing that.

Dad: We were in DeWitt during the time of racial strife. Although there were differences, we held fast to our Christian faith. Edward Bradford [an African American] was our custodian and became a great friend. His daughter, Barbara, helped Lois with housekeeping and babysat for us. One of Edward's sons was able to attend the University of Arkansas at Pine Bluff with the help of some of our friends from Tulsa, friends from my days as minister in Ozark (Dr. Duane and Sue Brothers). We have lost touch with him, but he was planning to be a school teacher.

Ron: Those kinds of little things – like you and Mother insisting that we call him Mr. Edward instead of Edward like most of the other kids (and adults) did, and having Barbara sit in the front seat of the car instead of the back seat – might have had a more profound, albeit subtle, effect on us than the racial crisis around whether or not to seat black visitors in the church.

Dad: DeWitt was the only town of the five we are journeying to where Lois didn't give birth to a son. Because of that I believe that it was a place where our family began to blossom. The little ones entered school; David entered high school; everyone was growing up. At Christmastime we used to decorate our front door in red with letters Lois stenciled, saying "McDonald Boys Town." We were proud of our family and the church and certainly enjoyed our four years in DeWitt.

Ron: So, Dad, are you saying that having a baby was a bad thing? I think you've forgotten how difficult teenagers could be – and would be! I think when we were teens we took some of those blossoms off the family tree for a while.

But that happened in Rogers.

Chapter Nine

ROGERS

July 21, 1998

Two days ago Dad and I journeyed to Rogers for our last church presentation. Once again it was an unforgettable experience. Dad told me as I left Conway for home Sunday night, "Ron, there's nothing you could have given me that would have been more meaningful than this experience. This has helped me tie up some loose ends in my ministry that I couldn't have done otherwise."

Then he added, "I think your ministry is very important. I love you."

An hour later, on the road home, I suddenly thought, "That sounded like his last words to me." A wave of sorrow rolled over me, anticipating his dying, followed by a deep, inward smile, for how could a son have a greater blessing bestowed upon him then those parting words?

Our journey began early last week when Dad called and we talked about our ideas on what to say. He said, "I've been thinking of the many things we did in Rogers as well as the new experiences that I had. We did a lot for the poor and less fortunate there. We started a day care center, a kindergarten, the youth group you were in. Those things were new for a church to do. Some didn't like it, either. They complained about bringing poor people into our facilities. Most were really supportive, though. It was a good church.

"I probably enjoyed Rogers more than any other church and town we lived in. You boys were older and blossoming. Mark was born there. David Driver joined us there. Joyce Ann (a foster child) lived with us. We had a wonderful experience there.

"Do you remember the paintings I had in my office in the church?" he asked me. "They were given to me by a prostitute who came to me for counsel. That was really new for me. Many people came to me for help while I was minister there."

I replied, "I've often thought of your work in Rogers as beginning the prime years of your ministry. DeWitt had been a place that challenged you to take a tough stand and helped your vision of the church to grow beyond local issues, but Rogers was where you were most innovative and where your preaching really deepened."

He agreed: "I had some great mentors there who helped me do things carefully and effectively. Plus, as you know, those who came to me for counsel had a lot to teach me."

We talked on and settled on a biblical text for our mutual theme: "Truly I say unto you, in as much as you have done it unto the least of these my brothers and sisters, you have done it unto me."

On Saturday morning I rose and did some house chores, then left for Conway. Dad, Mother, and I left their house around two o'clock together. Soon our conversation revolved around our thoughts about the coming service.

For me, knowing this will be our last trip together on this pilgrimage gave it extra emotional importance. In many ways our experience together has been moving much like Dad's ministry and my growth through these years of our lives together. Now we were in a sort of rhythm. We had a sense of what this was about. Dad turned 40 a few weeks before we moved to Rogers. He was entering the peak of his ministerial career. I was 13, just discovering my identity.

As a community Rogers wasn't as immediately welcoming and friendly as DeWitt had been, something we chalked up to the difference between the deep southern ways of DeWitt and the more reserved ways of the Arkansas hills. Within a week of moving there, however, my brother, Don, and I went to a Boy Scout camp on the Buffalo River that connected me with a friend for life, Jim Swearingen. Jim and I played sports together, did Scouting together, partied together, and sang together at church. I called him Friday night and invited myself to his house on Saturday evening to visit. Despite the fact that he was going to have to miss the Rogers service on Sunday, he wanted to visit as much as I did.

Rogers had grown from the mere 5000 people when we lived there to around 35,000. The church, in response, had struggled through a split that had created two thriving churches. Central United Methodist had moved to a large, new plant away from the old building we had attended, but some members of Central had decided to stay back at the downtown building and ministry there and start a new church, called First United Methodist Church. We had convinced the ministers of the two churches, Bobby Bell and Rodney Steele, to join together Sunday night so we could lead them in worship. Dad had been District Superintendent to both preachers, and was particularly close to Bobby, so he did the arrangements this time. Dad said the split had been painful and somewhat divisive, although both churches seemed stronger than ever. Our worship service could be a step in the direction of some healing of those old wounds. In fact, it might be the first such gathering of the two churches since the split.

Ron McDonald

I found an interesting contrast with our aborted trip to DeWitt. The DeWitt church had struggled internally not to split apart under Dad's ministerial leadership, while Rogers was a church where we might be a part of a ministry of reconciliation after a painful split. I couldn't help but think of the contrast between the prophetic stance Dad took in DeWitt and the position of comforter and acknowledgment of rebirth we found ourselves in at Rogers. In the prophetic tradition the prophet challenges and calls the people to new places, new ideas; then when the people move and change, the prophet ministers to their pain and hardship, helping them reconcile with what has been made new.

Our plan was to stay at a motel near Elm Springs, the town and church where my brother, Mark, was minister, and spend Sunday morning worshiping with Mark and his family.

Everyone of the boys in my family considered going into the ministry. David decided not to after a year of college. I decided to, changed my mind, changed again, and have reluctantly stayed in the ministry. Don decided to and changed his mind. Tom was in lay ministry for a while, then went on to become a writer. Jim was on the verge when he lived at a Wesley Foundation while in college, but went into social work administration. Mark, like me, wrestled with the ministry while staying with it. David Driver was a minister until his death. All of us are testaments to Dad's enormous influence over our perspective on life in community. Despite the fact that only two of us remain in professional ministry, every one of us is in the helping or activist professions.

I believe that our experiences in DeWitt and Rogers convinced us all that the church and a local minister are vital to the strength of a community. Despite the fact that the church is often not a social leader—sometimes even a roadblock to change—when the church and its ministers become leaders, they can truly change a community to the better. Dad learned the courage it takes to be a leader in DeWitt, that one sometimes has to be willing to stand alone even while working hard to maintain strong, trusting relationships. In Rogers he was able to cash in on that wisdom, build good relationships, and take on issues that were confronting a society in need of some flexibility.

During those years, society was changing radically, and the church had to either disassociate itself from those changes, hang onto old ways (which often made its positions irrelevant), or it had to find ways to adjust and keep faith in the foreground. People needed strength and courage to move with changing times. Dad tried to lead the DeWitt and Rogers churches in the second direction, accepting changes and then influencing it to move in the right direction.

I wondered as we drove up to Rogers if we would find the Rogers churches to be focused on feel-good religion and building church-growth empires, or would they be churches that sought to help people be inclusive and leaders for justice. The church-growth movement, like corporate consolidation, is about creating greater efficiency and magnetism, but at the expense of a truly prophetic message. Some may argue that the mega-churches—the so-called "successful" churches—are successful because of their prophetic message, but I think their messages are essentially mainstream, centrist affirmations. They are basically finding their niche in co-opting the dominant culture. Thus, you don't see many leaders from such churches emerging who look differently, act differently, and are calling for radical change. Not that change is inherently good, for sometimes it isn't. But change is necessary in a society where many, many people are left out of its riches. There will always be a place for radicals (a radical is one who goes to the root), and mega-churches simply don't nurture radicals.

Late Saturday I called Jim Swearingen and drove to Rogers to visit. I arrived before Jim had returned home from a supper with his brother, and with the extra time I went for a drive and walk around the old town, visiting my old schools and familiar neighborhoods. Two changes were obvious. Most things were bigger, like the whole town, and the town was now multicultural, filled with Latinos. When I had lived there, there were two cultures, period: middle class whites and poor whites.

Soon Jim arrived back home and he and I sat down to talk. It was such an engaging conversation that he neither offered nor did I ask for something cold to drink. For two hours we caught up on years of disconnected lives. I decided to ask him about what had happened with the church split: "Jim, Dad said the split of the two churches was pretty tough. What really happened?"

"I just didn't feel right about it, and when I went to Bobby Bell he just kept saying 'Deal with it.' I couldn't very well.

"Bobby was pretty intent on us moving, and my architectural firm even made a preliminary study on what we might build at what cost. It kept getting bigger and bigger. Bobby clearly had big plans. We wrestled with it a lot, and when the church voted to move, it barely passed, like 51% to 49%. There was some strong support for the move, but, looking back, I think we shouldn't have moved so fast after such a close vote.

"I kept feeling worse and worse about it. I felt we were leaving behind an important downtown ministry that I had invested years of my life into.

"One day at a ballgame I was talking with a friend who said, 'Jim, I'm just not sure if I can make this move with the church. I may just go to another church.' I replied, 'To tell you the truth, I'm thinking of the same thing.'

"The more we talked, the more we realized we were both surrounded by a number of friends who were feeling the same way. So we decided to have a meeting to discuss our options. We put out the word, and on a rainy night, 160 people showed up!

"Ron, I've never experienced a meeting like that one. We spent a couple of hours together with everyone expressing their pain and misgivings about leaving the old building and ministry behind. It was deeply moving. We left there with a plan to meet again in two weeks with a few of us assigned to write a mission statement for the possibility of creating a new church.

"Two weeks later, it was sleeting, but 170 people showed up, and we had another meeting like the first. I really felt the Spirit was moving among us. We decided to petition for a new church. Bobby was really against it and was pretty mad, but I don't think he knew how painful this was for many of us. He seemed to just want us to learn to live with the move, and we couldn't."

I said, "Sometimes I've noticed that when churches grow they often push forward without enough unity to make a smooth move. Things move forward that way, but those churches often lose many members while gaining a number of new people from the larger community. Maybe Bobby was so sure that the church needed to move on that he didn't see the importance of some of the things you were concerned about."

"I think so," Jim replied. "And he may have been right about what Central needed to do, but it just didn't feel right to us. We felt like there was a vital ministry at the old church that we shouldn't abandon. Bobby kept pushing ahead without us feeling like going along.

"This has really changed my view of what faith is about. Now I think faith is about trust or letting God act. Those early meetings were amazing to me. The spirit among us was so incredible, and we got things done that we could hardly believe were possible."

"In the Quaker tradition," I said, "those kinds of meetings are called 'gathered meetings.' Those are times when a half-dozen or more in attendance are clearly in the same spiritual place. It's very powerful."

"Then those were gathered meetings. They sure changed me."

We talked on, particularly about our shared experiences in high school and the church. At one point I told Jim that I often think of him whenever I find myself singing an old Methodist hymn in harmony. He and I used to sit at the back of the sanctuary and sing the bass harmony together.

He told me another story: "When I graduated from college, I got a job with an architectural firm in Little Rock that assigned me to Pine Bluff. We were doing some work on an antebellum house in DeWitt for a Miss Hattie Boone Black."

"She lived across the street from us," I offered.

He went on, "I told her that my home minister had been the pastor in DeWitt. She asked, 'Who was that?' I said, 'Charles McDonald.' She suddenly got stern and said, 'That man just about ruined that church. He wanted to bring niggers in.'

"I was young and new at the job, so I didn't say anything. But I sure wanted to!"

I asked, "What would you say if that happened to you now?"

"I would say that the two most influential men in my life were..." Suddenly my friend, Jim, choked up and began to cry. He haltingly choked out the remainder of the sentence: "...my father and Charles McDonald."

I sat quietly with him for a minute or so, then said, "I'll share with Dad what you said."

Jim had been the driving force behind Dad being honored by having the church fellowship hall named after him and my mother about 10 years before. Now I understood why.

I played Jim and his wife a tune on my dulcimer just to show off, then I left for Elm Springs.

On Sunday morning I awoke early, went for a run in a section of Arkansas that I used to run miles and miles in. It brought back so many memories of my younger days when my forays through the countryside was a sort of preparation for the wider adventures I would continue to have. So many of our childhood and youth experiences are playful preparations for the more independent, serious adventures of our adult lives. So many of my adventures were set in motion in those early years. We were so physical. My brother, Don, and I played nearly every sport together until we got thoroughly hooked on running. It was in running that we found the strength to go anywhere. It was that leg strength that has carried me into many forests, up many mountains, and over many, many roads. My ability as a runner gave me confidence that I couldn't have found any other way. I joke with my family that I'm confident that I can always run from a conflict, but there is some truth to that. If I were in danger I would still seek a way to run out of harm's way. Kind of like Forrest Gump, I guess.

I'll never forget the way I got hooked on running. I first ran to get in shape for basketball, and we were told we had to run in a cross country race for training. I began with my basketball teammates, running slowly at the back of the pack, until about half-way. At that point I began to feel better, while most runners around me slowed down. I nonchalantly picked up the pace, and by the end of the race I had come in second on the cross country team. I ran pretty well that fall, but it wasn't until the spring that I realized running might be my best sport.

One afternoon early in the spring track season in Rogers when I was a high school junior, Coach Lewellen told me and the other middle distance runners to run a half mile time trial. One of the runners, Ike Skaggs (now a coach and teacher of my son at Central High School in Memphis), was a gifted and determined runner, as well as a senior, probably the best runner on the team, and certainly the team leader. Like all the other runners, when we started the run I filed in behind Ike. Unlike the other runners, however, I wasn't fully aware of how good Ike was, and, without that knowledge to discourage me, I stayed with him through the whole run while the other runners dropped off the pace. I finished alongside of him. It didn't seem particularly hard to me.

Coach Lewellen came up to us after we had caught our breath and asked Ike, "Skaggs, what did you run that in?"

Ike, who was carrying the watch, said, "2 minutes 8 seconds."

Unbeknownst to me, that is an excellent high school half-mile time, especially early in the year, especially by a runner who had never run a half-mile for time before. So Coach Lewellen glanced at me, and looked incredulously at Ike, and asked again, "What did you *really* run it in?"

"2:08, Coach," Ike replied.

"You must have cut the corners," Coach said, glancing sideways at me again.

"No, Coach, we ran the whole thing."

"Then you must have started the clock late."

"No, Coach," Ike said, now with raised voice, "we ran an honest 2:08!"

Coach Lewellen looked suspiciously at me, then barked at Ike, "Don't talk back to me!" He walked away with a slight smile on his face.

I knew I was a runner!

I finished my run, and finding Dad in the pool, jumped in with him. I told him of my conversation with Jim, and he told me the part of the church story he had heard.

"It was a difficult decision, one that was maybe made too quickly.

"When I was a District Superintendent I once presided over a situation similar when a church barely voted to build another building. The vote was so close that I asked a couple of the church leaders to talk privately with me. They were worried enough about the decision that I said, 'I think it's best to take some more time with this, and so you don't have to take the heat, I'm going to veto it.' I went back out and carefully explained my decision, and the congregation applauded!

"I thought the District Superintendent should have done the same thing with the Central vote. It was just too close. He thought it was best not to move forward, but he didn't take a stand and veto it.

"Bobby, I think, was hurt by the split. The first meeting Jim told you about was during his vacation, and he probably felt betrayed. In spite of that, however, both churches are doing great. There's been some anger and hurt feelings, but I think God has worked with both churches.

"Our service will be the first joint service they've had since the split. Maybe it will help with some healing that needs to take place."

We worshiped at Elm Springs United Methodist Church, listening to Mark preach. He's an excellent preacher, a good teacher and storyteller.

What grabbed me the most, however, was the fact that the last time I worshiped at Elm Springs David Driver was the preacher. David joined our family while we were in Rogers. He was my older brother, David's, roommate at Hendrix. His father had abandoned his family, and his mother was mentally ill and committed in the state hospital. He graduated from Hendrix the same year I graduated from high school, 1969, and we invited him to spend the summer with us working at a factory with me. Our family and David hit it off well enough that he kept spending vacations with us throughout the rest of his life, and we claimed him as one of us. His joining of our family was not only a blessing to us and him, but it also was a clear statement of our family's openness to others. The more I thought about it, the more I believe that inclusiveness was the central theme of Dad's ministry, and David Driver represented that theme on a personal level.

We drove to Rogers in the late afternoon, Mother, Dad, and I. Dad and I both confessed that we were nervous, much like we had been at each church. Upon arriving Mother and Dad immediately recognized a few people, who introduced themselves to me as well. With each person there were descriptions of our mutual connections, but I didn't find myself feeling excited about being there until I met my old dentist, Dr. Russell Riggs, and his wife. Though they looked 30 years older, which they were, I easily recognized him.

Home Again

What a wonderful thing it is to see old friends 30 years later. All those body changes and wrinkles, but the same basic appearance, weathered with wisdom and experience. We laughed as we remembered that I had cleaned his office for $5 a week for about a year. He confessed, "I didn't pay you much, that's for sure. It was hard to earn a living as a dentist back then." I replied, "The pay was as good as any other job I had at that age." Then I confessed, "Besides, when I got tired of the job, I just stopped coming by. I guess I wasn't mature enough to say 'I quit.'"

We sat down next to Bobby Bell, who was quite an impressive man. Dressed casually, he was warm, open, and carried himself with a great deal of confidence and charisma. I liked him immediately.

My brothers, Mark and Jim, came with us, and when we started singing, we spontaneously invited Mark to sing a couple of songs with us. He's got quite a good voice. As he came forward Dad remarked, "He's the young punk who was born while we were here. The day we found out Lois was pregnant with Mark we spoke to all the boys at supper one night, saying, 'Boys, we have something to tell you.' Immediately Jim blurted out, 'Mother's going to have a baby!' We still haven't figured out how he knew!

"Ron wandered off into a room by himself and sat for an hour. That wasn't like Ron to sit still for an hour. I guess it just had to sink in."

After we sang "Trampin'" and "Swing Low, Sweet Chariot," I shared a long overdue confession.

> The room to my right off the balcony used to have a ladder that went up to an attic that led to the bell tower. To get onto it you had to walk across a plank that kept you from stepping onto the plaster ceiling and falling through. I had gone up there with Dad's

permission a few times, but he had told me not to go up there with other people.

But...Tom Playford, a friend of mine, and I were double dating one night and decided to check out the church bell tower with our dates. Back then you could get into the church using a clothes hanger—and we kept one hanging near the basement door. You could pop the lock real easily.

"I didn't want to know this!" Dad cried out to much laughter.

So we popped the lock and told the girls we wanted them to see what Rogers looked like from above. Dad had always wanted us to see things from above, so we figured we were doing what he wanted. We went up there (I pointed to the room next to the balcony in front of me) and climbed up the ladder. I went up first to show the girls where to go, and pointed the way towards the roof door, but I forgot to tell the girls to walk on the plank. One of them walked on the plaster. She busted a hole in it, fell through, and all that kept her from hitting the floor maybe 15 feet below was that she grabbed onto a rafter and hung on for dear life. Tom, down below, threw chairs out of the way so he might be able to catch her if she fell. I reached for her, but was clearly in such an awkward position that I didn't think I could pull her up. I said, "I don't have any leverage. I can't pull you up!" She wailed, "What am I going to do? What am I going to do?"

I didn't know!

Then, suddenly she changed her tune, screaming, "I'm slipping!!!" I reached down and, assisted by one of those adrenaline rushes, simply pulled her up like she didn't weigh a thing.

Home Again

We climbed back down and looked at this big hole where she had fallen through. My arms were shaking, my hands were a bit sore from the strength I'd used that I didn't know I had. Mainly, though, I was wondering how to tell Dad.

Some of y'all may know about that hole.

I didn't tell Dad that night, but the next morning was Sunday—it was a Saturday night problem. You know, that's when those kinds of things happen. I went into the sanctuary before church to see Dad. I said, "Dad, I gotta tell you something." I told him what had happened, sure that I'd get into some big trouble. All he said was, "Ron, I'm disappointed in you." Those words went through me like a knife. I think I grew up a lot at that moment.

Last night Jim Swearingen told me that when they were putting the steeple up there somebody remarked that the workers putting up the steeple knocked a hole in the ceiling right there.

Later I told Dad what Jim had told me and he said, "I went to Cecil Miller and Harold Wardloe, told them about it and said I'd be happy to pay for it out of my own pocket. They said, 'Don't worry about it, Charles, we'll take care of it.'"

Now that y'all have fixed it, if you still have a bill, you know where to send it. He said he'd pay for it! I was too young to have to pay for that kind of thing, right?

After a good laugh, Dad spoke next.

When we came here in 1965 it was a joyful time for us. We moved here with five sons and we left with seven. It was a growing time for our family, but it was a difficult time in the life of our nation. It was difficult for many families and many young people as they faced the problem of the war in Vietnam.

We lived at the old parsonage on Poplar and Dixieland. We put a wall where the garage door was and, as Russell Riggs reminded us, we called it a dormitory. Four or five of our sons stayed out there while we were here.

[My brother, David, brought a Jewish friend of his home for Christmas once. Glen Fleetwood was a gentle soul who smoked, something we playfully scorned. One cold night we threw his cigarettes out the back door onto the driveway. Glen quickly ran outside in his underwear to get them. As quickly as he ran out, we shut the door and locked it. He knocked and begged for us to let him in. So we said, "Only if you can say 'Rubber baby buggy bumpers' without a mistake." He did, easily. Too easily, so someone said, "You have to sing 'Jesus loves me.'" Glen was quiet for a few seconds, then we heard him say, "Rubber baby buggy bumpers." We laughed and let him in.]

Northwest Arkansas was just starting to grow to where it is now. Then there were only small towns, not the 250,000 people here now. The first Walmart store was established while we were here in Rogers. Daisy Air Rifles was here; Emerson Electric was established at that time; Wendt-Sonis Tool and Die Company was here. As Rogers grew, the church began to grow with it. Now there are five United Methodist Churches here in Rogers. It thrills us to read about the outreach ministries of these churches in your newsletters.

When we were here this church was a church that reached out, just as they do now. We started the Day Care Center downstairs in the basement for working mothers and their children We also started a Day Care

Home Again

Center at the Presbyterian Church, and a kindergarten at the Christian Church. We started a United Youth Fellowship of Methodists, Presbyterians, Disciples of Christ, and Episcopalians, a vital and enjoyable program for us to work with. It was a time when the church was reaching out to people of all ages—and a joyful time for us.

While we were here Dr. Ernie Dixon, President of Philander Smith College and later a bishop in the United Methodist Church, came here to preach in our church, bringing his family with him. He had a booming voice and contagious laughter. We really enjoyed it. He stayed at our house, ate with us, and the family attended Sunday School and worshipped with us. Bishop Dixon preached a great sermon, and as I was standing at the back door after worship, one of our dear friends from Mississippi said to me, "Charles McDonald, I never did think we'd have a colored person preach at our church, but he did a good job!" It lifted my heart. I had thought she was really going to get onto me.

I had the opportunity a few years later to vote for Ernie Dixon to become a bishop. He was elected and made a great bishop for us.

The Methodist churches in Rogers have always been family oriented. I learned while here to listen and be open to people who hurt.

The music program was great. Some of you may remember Joe Boyd, our choir director, along with our organists, Leon Warren, Linda Harris, and Betty Sutton on the piano. The music program was inspiring, and it still is. Many of you remember the wonderful music at annual conference from the choir at Central Methodist Church.

I'm grateful to you for helping me to learn and grow while we were here.

The scripture Ron read says, 'In as much as you have done it unto the least of these, my brothers and sisters, you have done it unto me.' In the Sunday School lesson today in *The Mature Years*—I read it now, because I'm finally mature!—the writer, John Gooch, said that the Bible is an interesting mixture of teaching of how we relate to God and how we must relate to one another. He reminded us of a song sung in the '50s that said 'You can't have one without the other—love and marriage go together.' The Bible makes it clear that we have to love God and we have to love one another. I learned this from the Bible, particularly the prophets of the Old Testament.

I had a professor in seminary, Dr. Hicks, who could hardly see. He'd hold the Bible right up to his face and read in his bellowing voice from the prophets. I can still see him in my mind's eye, as if he were one of the prophets. He talked about what Amos said: "Justice must roll down like waters in an unending stream." He talked about Hosea and the God of love—the God that reaches out. Hosea reached out to his wife Gomer and loved her in spite of the fact that she had left him for another man. He talked about the prophets and made us understand that they were saying that justice and love must prevail in our world—then and today. Then he spoke for Isaiah and sounded like Isaiah when he went up on a high mountain and said, 'Here comes our God!' And Jesus came.

Dr. Wesley Davis, our New Testament professor, helped us to understand that Jesus teaches us how to live, and how to love, and how to serve. He was an inspiration to me, for he helped me to understand that

Home Again

the way of Jesus is a way of love, a way of service, a way of reaching out to people, of listening to people, of loving people, and helping people where they are. That's what we try to do in the United Methodist Church.

"In as much as ye have done it unto these, my brothers and sisters, ye have done it unto me," Jesus said.

I learned that love is all important: love of God, love of church, love of family, and love for all God's children.

In my notebook that I don't carry that often anymore — I don't preach much anymore — I have these words: 'These are my friends. They would see Jesus.' At the bottom I have these words: 'The Gospel is the gospel of the second chance.' For God gives us a chance again and again to share the love we find in Christ that we might live and love and serve like Jesus. This is the message we need to hear again and again — that God's love reaches out to us, and that we are a part of that love, share in that love today and everyday.

"In as much as ye have done it unto these, my brothers and sisters, ye have done it unto me," says the Lord.

Amen.

Dad looked at me, went to his seat, and as he sat down, I rose to speak.

I have sat over there where the Riggs are sitting time and time again and heard my father preach — and sometimes I even listened. We've had an extraordinary journey. This town and church is the climax or end of our shared journey as father and son, because from here I went on off to college, to seminary, and became a pastoral counselor.

When our family lived in DeWitt, Dad and Mother had often talked about how people are people; it doesn't matter whether you are white or black.' But the waves of the Civil Rights movement were rolling through the South. It wasn't felt as much here in Rogers, except for the questions being raised about signs in town that said no black person could spend the night here in Benton County. But the real movement and conflict was in places like DeWitt.

There, the Official Board considered a resolution to not seat colored people if they came to our church. Dad felt compelled to take a stand against such a resolution; and it was not an easy one to take. It shook us all up, made everyone in our family think and think about how we include people who look different, and how much do we put ourselves on the line for such convictions. We watched our father struggle though that, found ourselves sometimes ostracized from certain social circles.

Two years later we moved to Rogers, a church whose ministry took on an inclusiveness that has deeply influenced me. I could see that what happened in DeWitt made Dad define his convictions with courage, so when he came here he had discovered his own mettle. He found here a church that also had the mettle to let poor people come into this church in the Day Care Center. While many churches were saying, "Why don't the mothers just stay home and take care of their children?" this church thought it should provide a day care center for the working poor.

Dad tells one story about a woman who came to him for counsel, confessing that she was a prostitute.

Home Again

She kept visiting him and gave him paintings she had painted. On his walls he hung two pictures painted by a prostitute — a Mary Magdalene of Rogers.

This church was a church that was allowing people in who needed to be here. It was an inclusive church. So when I went off to college and worked at Aldersgate Camp and had two roommates who were black, I didn't think twice about it. I know why I didn't, too. I didn't have to. My parents had done that thinking for me. It was second nature for me think, 'What's the big deal?' Now my kids say that to me about some of the things I struggle with, helping to broaden my life. I had roommates, but my children have best friends of different races.

My ministry to the working poor has its roots here in Rogers. Not only that, but this ecumenical youth ministry that began here and met in Bill Rail's church most of the time was of enormous influence on me. The youth group here was founded because of the strong ministerial relationships Dad had with Bill Rail and Ernie O'Donnell and their concern that they didn't have enough youth to create a strong youth group. We had enough Methodist youth, but we shared our strength, and it made us all stronger. We didn't push Methodism, but we pushed Christianity here. We taught character.

When my son was in the seventh grade I thought of the Rogers youth group and knew I wanted him to have a similarly good experience with church youth. I established an ecumenical, interracial youth group with programs like the ones we had here, and they kept coming back. I've run it for 8 years now.

We once took a trip to Washington D.C., our white and black kids, and sat on the steps of the Lincoln

Memorial where Martin Luther King gave his 'I Have a Dream' speech and read the entire speech — two paragraphs each — as people gathered around us to hear this realization of King's dream. I was blessed to be a part of that.

I believe that began right here in Rogers, in these churches that had and, I hear, still have an inclusive ministry.

Sometimes we meet people who change the way we think about life. I've met people here and all sorts of places. One in particular was a woman who came to me as her pastoral counselor and gave me permission to tell this story publicly.

She came in, sat down, and said, "Dr. McDonald, I need your help. I've lost my soul."

I asked, "How did that happen?"

She said, "I grew up in a harsh family, poor, with little support from my parents. When I was 18 I got pregnant out of wedlock. I thought about getting an abortion, but I couldn't do that. I decided to have the child. I debated whether to give the child away for adoption or keep it myself. I drew a line down a piece of paper, and on one side I wrote, 'Keep the Child.' On the other I wrote, 'Give the Child Away.' On the side labeled, 'Keep the Child, there were only one or two reasons. On the other side, the side labeled, 'Give the Child Away,' the list reached the bottom of the page. So I decided to give the child away for adoption.

"But I was poor, and the doctors didn't know me personally, and upon giving birth to the child, instead of taking her away from me and informing the adoption people, they laid the child on my lap and left me alone in the room with my baby for over a hour. I bonded with my baby immediately like some mothers

Home Again

do. I had never felt so much love in all my life. I even named her. I felt so alive and caring.

"Then they came back into the room, apologized for their mistake, and took my baby away for adoption. When they took that baby from me I gave away my soul.

"I have lived a hard life since then. I haven't been bad, but I'm not proud of myself. I've had a lot of relationships and problems. I'm an alcoholic—but I'm in recovery now. I've never worked a day time job. I've always worked at night. I've never had a soul.

"They told me, though, that I could contact my daughter when she turned 18, which she did recently. I felt that I could get my soul back when I saw her again.

"But they've change the rules.

"Now she has to be 21 before I can reach out to her.

"I have three more years to wait, and I don't think I can make it. I'm falling apart."

I knew from my years of counseling with people that it probably wouldn't help for me to simply reassure her that she'd be OK, even if I believed it. That's the front door, and people truly live nearer the back door where they listen most deeply to stories. So I told this story, one that you know, too.

"There were these two women prostitutes who lived just outside of town in a tent. They both had little babies of the same age. They were ostracized during the day. They only worked at night, the only time men would come see them. They were drunks, too.

"One night one of the women went to bed so drunk that she rolled over onto her baby. She was so drunk that she did not feel her baby struggle for air. She did not feel the baby's muffled cries. She smothered her own child to death. When she awoke the next day and found her baby dead, she was so horrified and grief stricken, she impulsively switched her dead child for the child of her friend, who was still asleep.

"When the other woman awoke and found a dead baby beside her, she too was horrified, but she recognized that the baby was not her own and found her baby being nursed by her friend. She said, 'You've switched the babies!' Her friend denied this, and they began to argue so vehemently that they drew a crowd.

"No one could help resolve the conflict, because they didn't know one child from the other. They had avoided the women, or couldn't admit that they hadn't.

"So they took those two mothers and the live baby to King Solomon. King Solomon listened to their stories, called for a swordsman and said, 'Cut that baby in half. Give half to one mother and half to the other.' And the mother whose baby had died, scornfully said, 'Good.' But the true mother screamed, 'No! No! Give the baby to her! I'd rather my baby live with her than to die!'"

I sat quietly for a few moments and looked at the woman before me. She was transfixed in tears. Gently, I said, "King Solomon knew the true mother, for he knew that he was in the presence of someone who would give her own soul away so that her baby could live."

We sat there in silence while she quietly wept. I knew she understood what I had said to her. Finally, I spoke through my own tears, "It's not often that I am in the presence of someone who has such nobility that she would be willing to give her own soul away so that her child could live."

Home Again

I looked at the quiet congregation before me and said, "Would that you and I had that kind of nobility, that we would be willing to give our own souls away so that someone else could live.

"In many ways some of you do have such nobility. Some of your soul is in me. The souls of all of us are mixed together. It is our job, as Dad says, to love so much that we would give our own souls away so that we can all live.

"So I'm here today to thank you for giving some of your soul to me, because I'm alive and glad I am back here in this wonderful church, in this wonderful town, with this wonderful ministry that keeps giving its soul away to the least of these our brothers and sisters."

After worship we left the sanctuary and visited with folks in the Fellowship Hall, built under Dad's leadership and named for Mother and Dad: "Charles and Lois McDonald Hall". It wasn't a particularly meaningful reception for me, for there really weren't many there whom I remembered well. I was disappointed in that, but I was touched by John Swearingen's (Jim's father) gratitude for our message—he thanked me from his heart.

We conversed quietly as we drove back to Conway, noting that our pilgrimage was over. It had been an amazing experience, and it seemed that words couldn't express its full meaning. As I left Conway to travel back to Memphis the next day, Dad hugged me and said, "Ron, I think you could not have given me anything greater than this gift. This has been very special to me, and you certainly have an important ministry yourself. Thank you."

I don't remember what I said.

I don't think it mattered.

I know what I felt, and that mattered.

About The Author

Dr. Ron McDonald is a Quaker and pastoral counselor at the Church Health Center in Memphis, Tennessee, a nationally recognized medical facility for the working uninsured. He was born and raised in Arkansas, the son of a United Methodist minister and his wife, Charles and Lois McDonald. Ron became a Quaker in 1979 and has been presiding Clerk of the Memphis Friends Meeting. He was educated at Hendrix College in Conway, Arkansas, Union Theological Seminary in New York City, Saint Paul School of Theology in Kansas City, Missouri, and the Training Institute for Counseling and Therapy of the Foundation for Religion and Mental Health in Braircliff Manor, New York. He is a Diplomate in the American Association of Pastoral Counselors and the author of *Building the Therapeutic Sanctuary: The Fundamentals of Psychotherapy – A Pastoral Counseling Perspective* (1stBooks, 2000).

Additionally, he is a folksinger and storyteller who performs with his guitar and hammer dulcimer. He is married to Susan Penn and together they have two sons.

Dr. McDonald's e-mail address is: mcdonaldr@churchhealthcenter.org

Printed in the United States
5507